# Max Is Missing!

### by Ben M. Baglio

## SCHOLASTIC INC.

New York  Toronto  London  Auckland  Sydney
Mexico City  New Delhi  Hong Kong  Buenos Aires

BooK

Special thanks to Lucy Courtenay

ISBN 0-439-68884-1

12 11 10 9 8 7 6 5 4 3 2 1          5 6 7 8 9 10/0

Printed in the U.S.A.

First Scholastic printing, January 2005

# Chapter One

Andi Talbot pushed her brown hair out of her eyes and stood back to admire the Pet Finders Club poster. She'd taped it onto the pet store window between an ad for birdseed and a newspaper clipping about gerbil care.

She bent down to stroke the golden cocker spaniel sitting beside her. "What do you think, Max?" she asked. "Should we ask the others?" Max blinked up at her with his soulful, chocolate brown eyes. Straightening up, Andi banged on the window to get her friends' attention, pointing to the poster and lifting up her hands to show that she wanted their opinion.

Out on the sidewalk, Natalie Lewis tipped her head to one side so that her shiny blond hair draped neatly over one shoulder. Then she came to the door of the pet store and put her head inside. "It's crooked," she announced.

1

"It is not!" Andi said indignantly. "It's perfect!"

Natalie shrugged. "If you think it's perfect, what are you asking me for?"

"Ask Tristan for me, will you?" said Andi. "He's just making faces through the glass."

"No change there," Natalie joked. She ducked outside again and prodded the red-haired boy kneeling on the sidewalk with the toe of her Mary Janes.

Tristan Saunders was tickling Andi's Jack Russell terrier, Buddy, who was lying on his back with his paws in the air. He looked up and narrowed his eyes critically at Andi's poster. "It has a kooky, homemade air," he shouted through the glass.

Andi rolled her eyes. "Enough already with the brochure-talk. This isn't one of your parents' real estate tours," she reminded him.

Tristan put his hands in the air. "What do you want me to say?" he complained dramatically. "You're always telling me I'm too bossy and you don't need my opinion on everything. Then when you *ask* me for it, you *still* don't want it. I can't win!"

Laughing, Andi climbed over Max and a stack of fabric-covered pet beds, and went outside to look at the poster. PET FINDERS CLUB, it read, in bold red letters on a white piece of poster board. Andi had scanned a cute picture of a dog underneath the title, followed by both her home and cell numbers at the bottom. *It looks terrific*, Andi thought. *But . . .*

"Okay, so it's crooked," she admitted. "Go and fix it, Nat."

"Hey!" Natalie protested, flicking her hair back and folding her arms. "Since when does the new kid get to tell me what to do?"

"Since right now," Andi retorted with a grin. Andi and her mom had moved all the way across the country three weeks earlier, from sunny Florida to Orchard Park, Seattle. When her mom got the job in Seattle, Andi was convinced that she'd hate it on the West Coast. She had to leave her school, her sprawling, sunshine-filled house by the sea, and worst of all, her best friend Jessica. They promised to e-mail each other, but Andi knew that it wouldn't be the same.

But so much had happened to Andi since the move that Florida was already starting to feel unreal. The new house was great, Fairfield Middle School was okay, and she could hardly believe that she'd only known Natalie and Tristan for a few weeks. *Best friends with a prom queen and a clown*, she thought wryly. *Life is full of surprises.*

A sudden burst of roadside drilling made Buddy leap

off the sidewalk and press against Andi's ankles. She scooped him up in her arms and tucked his little tan-and-white face under her chin.

"Is all of Main Street being dug up today?" Tristan coughed, flapping his hand to clear the dust.

Andi looked over her shoulder at the groups of workmen wearing bright orange vests, and the piles of rubble and digging equipment littering the street. "Looks like it," she said. "And on a Saturday, too. Don't those guys get a weekend?"

Natalie banged on the window and gestured toward the sign she was still holding up against the glass.

"Now *that's* perfect," Andi declared.

"The Pet Finders Club is official," Tristan announced, as Natalie came out of the store again.

Buddy squirmed in Andi's arms. She put him down and scratched him in the spot he loved, right between the ears. "And it's all thanks to you, Buddy," she said, smiling. "If you hadn't gotten lost the week we came to Orchard Park, I'd never have gone looking for you. . . ."

"And you'd never have met me. . . ." Tristan continued.

"And we'd never have started the club," Natalie finished with a grin.

It had been as simple as that. By looking for Buddy,

Andi had gotten to know Orchard Park like the back of her hand in just a few days. She'd met new people, found new hangouts, and settled in more quickly than she ever thought she would. And, most importantly, she realized that the people of Orchard Park needed her — and her new friends — to help them find their missing pets.

Suddenly, Max hurtled through the door of the pet store and raced past them, his silky golden ears flapping as he barked madly at a dirty white construction van that was driving past.

"Hey!" Andi exclaimed, sprinting after the over-excited spaniel. "What are you doing, you crazy dog? Come here!"

Buddy rushed ahead of Andi and quickly caught up with the runaway. Max skidded to a halt and barked playfully at the terrier. Seizing her opportunity, Andi caught Max by the collar and dragged him back toward the store, with Buddy close at her heels.

Max's owner, Christine Wilson, ran out of the store looking worried. She smiled gratefully when she saw Andi. "Thanks for grabbing him," she said. "He's crazy about cars, especially white ones. They remind him of the store van, and he always thinks we're about to go out for a drive."

She knelt down to clip a leash onto the spaniel, who barked and wagged his tail. "What am I going to do with you, Max?" Christine scolded gently. "I can't keep you locked upstairs, and I can't watch you all the time when you're in the store. You've got to be more sensible!"

"What do you think of the poster, Christine?" Tristan prompted.

"It's terrific," she said. "I'm glad Paws for Thought can help out with the publicity. I know how badly it hurts to lose a pet. One time, when Max was a puppy, he disappeared after digging a hole under the fence. I thought I'd lost him forever. Luckily, he was the only golden cocker spaniel in Orchard Park, so someone soon found him and brought him back." She gave Max an affectionate pat, and the elderly spaniel licked her hand. "I don't know what I'd do if I lost him again," Christine added quietly.

Andi knew exactly what she meant, because she'd felt like it was the end of the world when Buddy disappeared. She pressed her cheek against his smooth tan-and-white fur, feeling his little body squirm under her hands.

Christine checked her watch. "Okay then, we've got a lot to do before our first customers arrive — " she said, "cleaning out the cages and feeding everyone for starters. Ready for work, Tristan?"

"I prefer to think of it as a 'useful commercial experience,'" Tristan corrected her, following Christine into the store. "*Work* sounds too much like . . . work."

He had been helping out at the store for a couple of weeks now. With Christine being his mom's cousin, it was a great arrangement. He loved reptiles, and in between sweeping the floor and tidying the stockroom, he usually hung around the snake and lizard cages and read Christine's library of reptile books. His favorite new hobby was sharing snake facts with Andi and Natalie in the school cafeteria, saving the most gruesome parts for when they were taking the first bites out of their sandwiches.

"Do you want some extra help today, Christine?" Andi offered.

"It's the least we can do in return for letting us put a poster in the window," Natalie added.

"Thanks, guys! I know a good offer when I see one," Christine joked. "I'm always swamped on Saturdays, even with Tristan's help. Bring Buddy in, he can keep Max company."

Entering the store, Andi breathed in the comforting

smell of sawdust and dog biscuits, and listened to the loud squeaking and chirping coming from the cages. She loved it in here, with the cages stacked on shelves down one wall of the store, bags of feed at the back, and the other wall filled with long tanks of brightly colored fish. In between, every spare bit of space was piled high with things like rubber chews, flea collars, catnip mice, and rope toys.

Natalie started by feeding the fish. Tristan swept the floor, while Christine put prices on the new stock and tidied up the shelves. Andi collected some clean straw and sawdust from the back of the store and headed for the smallest cages. A small army of gerbils, chinchillas, rabbits, hamsters, and guinea pigs watched her with bright, unblinking eyes as she leaned into each cage and refreshed the bedding. In the cage closest to the window, her fingers brushed against the velvet-soft fur of a dove-gray, lop-eared rabbit. It snuffled its tiny pink nose and hopped away to the other side of the cage.

Tristan came over with a teetering stack of boxes in his arms. He began stacking them in the window. "Hey, Andi!" he whispered. "See that kid outside?" He nodded at a pale-faced boy of about eight, who was standing with his nose pressed up against the window. "He comes to see that gray rabbit every day. But you know what? He never comes inside."

The boy was leaning so close, he looked like he wanted to push his way through the glass. When Andi caught his eye, he went bright red and backed away.

"He looks scared to death," Andi said.

"That's because he's been looking at Tristan for the past two weeks," Natalie joked as she walked past with a broom and dustpan.

Tristan rolled his eyes. "Ha ha," he said. "Hey, Nat, have I told you about how a boa constrictor kills its prey? It winds around them and squeezes them to death — "

Natalie scowled and put up her hands to block her ears as she walked back toward the counter.

"Quit teasing her, Tristan. You know she hates snakes!" Andi scolded. "I'm going out to say hi to that kid. He probably needs a little encouragement to come through the door."

She went over to the door and stuck her head outside to give the boy her friendliest smile. "That's a pretty cool rabbit, isn't it?" she said. "Do you want to come in and take a look?"

The boy blushed again. "N-no, thanks," he stammered.

Andi pushed the door wider. "It's okay," she insisted. "No one's going to make you buy her. Christine — she runs the store — is really good about stuff like that. I just figured you'd like to pet her, maybe. Her ears are the softest things ever!"

The boy's eyes blazed with excitement. "Can I really pet her?" he breathed.

"Sure you can," Andi said. "My name's Andi, by the way. Who are you?"

"Liam," the boy whispered. He followed Andi into the store and stared wide-eyed as she leaned down to open the rabbit's cage. The rabbit stayed very still as Andi scooped her up and lifted her out of the cage. Liam very slowly reached out his hand, almost as if he was afraid to touch the rabbit.

"Liam! There you are!" A blond woman with a stroller was standing by the door. She looked tired and annoyed. "What are you doing? You know we can't have a rabbit. How many times have I told you?"

Liam snatched his hand back from the rabbit as if it were red hot. "I wasn't going to buy it, Mom," he protested.

His mom held out her hand toward him. "I'm sorry, honey," she said. "It's just not possible. I can't look after it when you're at school, and Lacey is still too young. She doesn't understand about pets."

Right on cue, the little girl in the stroller started crying. To Andi's surprise, Liam screwed up his face and rushed out of the store. "Why does everything have to be about Lacey all the time? It's not fair," Andi heard him shout over his shoulder as he ran down the street. "It's just not *fair*!"

# Chapter Two

"That poor kid," Andi said, feeling awful. "He really wants that rabbit, doesn't he? I guess I shouldn't have invited him inside. I think I just made things worse."

Tristan wasn't listening. His attention had shifted to something much more important, in his opinion. Christine was standing beside them with a plastic tub in her hand.

"Time to feed the reptiles," she announced.

"Can I — " Tristan began.

"No!" Christine said. "Tris, I know you want to handle the snakes, but I'm afraid that's one job I can't trust to anyone else. They're just too unpredictable."

Tiny geckos and bigger lizards clung to the sides of their glass tanks, watching with beady eyes as Christine approached with the food. In the next tank, three corn snakes basked under hot lamps. A garter snake caught

Andi's eye as it twisted around in yet another tank, showing off its glittering blue-black skin and flickering its neat tongue toward her.

Andi peered closer at one of the corn snakes. Unlike the others, the little reptile's coffee-colored skin looked dull and scaly, and she stayed curled up in a far corner of her cage as Christine filled up her water.

"That corn snake doesn't look too good," said Tristan, echoing Andi's thoughts.

"She's been quiet for a day or two," Christine agreed, looking worried. "I called Fisher, and he's coming to take a look at her this morning."

Fisher Pearce was a good friend of Christine's who worked for the ASPCA. It hadn't taken Natalie long to notice that Christine blushed whenever his name was mentioned, and to point this out to Andi in a loud whisper.

Tristan leaned as close as he could to the corn snake. "I've been reading about snake diseases," he said eagerly. "Maybe if I just took a look — "

Christine shook her head and laughed. "Tristan, you can't diagnose a snake just from reading a couple of books! Fisher's an expert, so I think we should wait for him, okay?"

"So I guess it's back to sweeping the floor then, " Tristan said with a sigh.

There was the sound of a van honking out back. Lifting his head from his sunning spot in the window, Max barked joyfully and pelted through the store as fast as his paws could take him. Buddy followed a minute later.

"Better than that," Christine said, looking in the direction of the sound, "Natalie can watch the register while you two help me unload that delivery of birdseed."

The van honked its horn again. When Andi and Tristan reached the yard, the delivery man was laughing out of his open window at Max, who was trying to leap into the driver's seat.

"See what I mean about white vans?" Christine said with a grin.

Andi grabbed Buddy's collar to keep him from joining in, while Tristan pulled Max away from the van. Then the delivery guy and Christine quickly unloaded the sacks of birdseed onto the ground.

"Never a dull moment around here," joked the delivery man, pausing to ruffle Max's ears before he got back into the van.

"Never a *quiet* moment either," said another voice, as the van drove out of the yard. Andi looked around and saw an elderly lady with curly, graying hair peering over the gate that led into the yard next door. "Really, Miss Wilson, that dog of yours is a real nuisance. Can't you control him better?"

"Morning, Mrs. Harper," Christine said cheerfully. "Sorry about all the noise. You know what Max is like when he sees a white van."

Mrs. Harper folded her arms across her fluffy violet sweater and looked at Max like he smelled bad. "That dog needs training. My poor customers can hardly hear themselves think."

"I'll try not to let it happen again," Christine promised, shooing Max back through the door of Paws for Thought. "Bye, Mrs. Harper."

"And another thing — " Mrs. Harper began, but Christine, Andi, and Tristan had scooped up the sacks of feed and fled back inside the store before she could finish.

"Phew!" said Christine, leaning against the door with relief. "I just don't have time to stand there and listen to her today."

"Why doesn't she like you?" Andi asked curiously, putting down her sack of birdseed. Buddy came over and sniffed at it hopefully.

"She just doesn't like the store much," Tristan

explained. "She's always worrying about snakes getting out and dogs barking and stuff."

"Running a pet store is a little different than managing a store full of tame embroidery silks and nice, quiet wool," Christine admitted with a sigh. "But it's not like any of my animals roam around loose — except Max, of course, and he wouldn't hurt a fly."

The store was getting busier now that it was nearly lunchtime. Andi went over to help a boy who was looking for a hamster. She lifted one of the warm little animals out of its cage and put it in the boy's hands. The boy's eyes brightened as he chose his hamster, and Andi decided that working in a pet store was a great job — almost as good as being a pet finder. Not that they'd had any cases since Buddy and Natalie's dog, Jet, got lost at exactly the same time a few weeks earlier. But now that the posters were up, Andi was sure it wouldn't be long before the phone was ringing off the hook with desperate owners wanting their pets tracked down.

An hour later, her feet were starting to ache and she was having second thoughts about working in a store. One woman had talked to her for ages, trying to choose a lizard. Andi found it hard to be enthusiastic about a pet that looked and acted like a stick of wood.

Andi blew her hair out of her eyes and grinned. "How does Christine manage when she's alone?"

Natalie winked. "Oh, I'm sure Fisher helps out when he can. I don't think he comes over just to see the animals, if you know what I mean." She nodded her head in Tristan's direction. "Have you heard what Tristan's talking about with that guy over there? Seriously gross!"

Tristan was deep in conversation with a short, sandy-haired man beside the reptile cages. "I wouldn't have a problem feeding them live rats or anything like that," he was telling the man earnestly. "It's natural, isn't it? I'd love a snake, but my mom would freak. What kind do you have?"

"All kinds," the sandy-haired man replied with a shrug. He didn't seem quite as interested in small talk as Tristan.

"The garter snakes are great," Tristan enthused, "but the one I'd really like is a python. Do you have a python?"

"Yeah, a couple. Listen, I gotta go. Great talking to you, kid." The sandy-haired man turned and started walking toward the door, bending down to give Max a pat on the way out.

"Come in any time," Tristan called after him. "Great to meet someone who understands — "

The door tinkled shut, and the rest of Tristan's sentence hung in the air.

"Bored another customer to death, I see," Natalie observed. Andi couldn't help laughing.

"He was really interested in the reptiles," Tristan protested. "You wouldn't understand."

The door opened again and a tall, handsome man came into the store, ducking slightly to avoid a birdcage.

"Morning all," he said, shrugging off his battered red backpack. He smiled at Christine, his teeth bright white against his dark skin. "How's it going?"

"Hey, Fisher. It's going great, thanks to this bunch." Christine nodded toward Andi and the others. "This is Fisher Pearce, guys, the veterinarian from the ASPCA."

"Hey there," said Fisher. "You must be the Pet Finders Club, right? I saw your poster in the window."

"Could we put one up at the ASPCA center, Mr. Pearce?" Andi asked, digging around in her bag for a poster.

"Call me Fisher," said the vet. "And of course you can." He took the poster from Andi and tucked it into his backpack. "I'll put it on the bulletin board in the reception area. My folks have told me a lot about you guys," he added. "Especially Tristan's love for banana brownies."

"Your parents are Maggie and Jango at the Banana Beach Café, right?" Andi guessed. "That place is great! I'm not surprised Tristan's banana brownie habit is famous around here."

Fisher laughed in agreement before turning to Christine. "So, who's the patient this time?"

Christine led him down to the corn snake's cage, with Andi and Tristan close behind. Natalie hung back, fiddling with her rainbow-colored friendship bracelet.

"Come and take a look, Nat!" Andi called over her shoulder. "The snake won't bite you. It's feeling too sick."

"I, er . . . I've got stuff to do up here," Natalie said, "like polishing the dog food cans."

"Chicken," Tristan scoffed.

Andi turned back to watch Fisher put on a pair of sturdy snake-handling gloves. He lifted the sickly corn snake out of its cage and took it over to the window to examine it in the light. Andi held her breath. What if it was serious? She knew that the reptiles were easily the most valuable animals in the store, and it would be a real shame if this one couldn't find a home.

"Nothing to worry about," Fisher said, putting the snake back in the cage and shutting the door. "This little lady is just getting ready to shed her skin. They

always look that way a few days before they slough it off."

"How does it come off?" Andi asked.

Tristan butted in before Fisher could even open his mouth. "The snake just crawls out of it like an old sock, and the new skin is all ready and waiting underneath."

The vet nodded, looking amused. "Uh, yeah. You got it. She'll be a bit soft and raw at first, so you should avoid handling her for a couple of days, Christine. Then she'll be gleaming and good as new."

"Excuse me!" said a shrill voice from the other end of the store.

They all looked around. The lizard-choosing lady was standing at the register. "I'm ready to buy my lizard now," she announced.

Christine hurried over. "Certainly, Mrs. . . . ?"

"O'Donnell," said the customer. "Do you need me to spell it?"

Christine shook her head. "No need, Mrs. O'Donnell. It's just good to know my customers' names."

"Two Ns, two Ls," Mrs. O'Donnell said, ignoring her. "If you write it down, be sure to spell it correctly."

She had chosen a bright green gecko with red markings on its back. Tristan put the gecko into a small straw-lined box while Christine rang up the purchase.

Mrs. O'Donnell picked up one of the Pet Finders Club flyers that were sitting by the register and examined it over the top of her glasses. "Pet Finders Club," she read out loud. "Who or what is the Pet Finders Club?"

Tristan gave Mrs. O'Donnell his best smile. "We are an exclusive association of keen-eyed animal lovers who offer a pet location service," he began. "We — "

"Find pets, I take it," Mrs. O'Donnell said dryly. "There's no need to sell it to me, young man. I've only just bought my gecko. I have no intention of losing it already."

Tristan went bright red.

"I trust that you are not just in it for the rewards?" the lady went on, raising her eyebrows. "It's not right, taking money from people in distress, you know."

Rewards! Andi exchanged a startled glance with Natalie. It hadn't occurred to her that people might want to offer them money.

"We hadn't even thought about that," she admitted. Then she had a realization. "But if any reward is offered, we'll give it to the ASPCA! Right, guys?"

Tristan looked horrified.

"Great idea, Andi," Natalie said mischievously, glancing at Tristan. "We'll pledge that on our next run of posters."

Fisher raised his eyebrows. "I'm impressed," he said. "In fact, I'll take a few more posters. I'll drop by again in a couple of days, Christine, to see how the corn snake is getting on."

Tristan groaned and shook his head as Fisher and Mrs. O'Donnell and her gecko left the store.

"What?" Andi protested, acting innocent. "We aren't in it for the money, are we?"

Beside her, Natalie tried to turn a giggle into a cough and failed.

Tristan gave a hollow laugh. "I can't believe you just pledged away all our funds!" he said. "What about our expenses?"

Natalie folded her arms. "Such as?"

"Photocopying," said Tristan after a pause, "computer ink, wear and tear on cycle wheels."

"*Tristan!*" Andi and Natalie burst out in unison and leaned over to nudge the red-haired boy on the arm.

"Hey!" Tristan said, holding out his hands to protect himself. "I'm just saying, you girls have got a *lot* to learn about business!"

# Chapter Three

Andi pressed the RECORD button on the phone.

"Hi, you've reached the Fet Pinders — oh, geez . . . "

She hit the STOP button again and took a deep breath. Maybe "hi" didn't sound professional enough, anyway. She had to stop trying so hard. She counted to five, then pressed RECORD again.

"Honey!" her mom called. "Buddy needs his breakfast, and we've got to go in five minutes!"

"You have reached the Pet Finders Club," Andi said quickly. "Please leave a telephone number and a brief description of your missing pet, and we'll call you back as soon as we can. And remember, you're not alone."

Andi was proud of that last part. She wanted people to know that the Pet Finders Club really cared about its customers. Natalie had said it made her sound like an alien nut.

Buddy barked just as she leaned down to press STOP. "Buddy!" Andi groaned. "Now I'll have to do it again!"

"I'm sure it's okay, honey," said Mrs. Talbot. "Buddy barked after you'd finished speaking, didn't he? I think it gives your message a personal touch." She applied some lipstick in the hall mirror and started putting on her coat. "You've got four minutes, and I'm out that door."

Andi quickly dug a can of dog food out for Buddy, poured it into a bowl, and set it down. "Can you check for any messages at lunchtime when you come home to walk Buddy, Mom?" she asked, leaning down to give her dog a good-bye pat before scooping up her school bag and slinging it over her shoulder.

"Sure, honey," her mom said absently. "But you'd better check them when you get home tonight as well, in case I forget."

"I'll pick up Buddy and double check the messages before I go over to Tristan's after school, then," Andi decided, hopping into the passenger seat and clipping on her seatbelt. Her mom worked until six o'clock on Mondays, so Andi was always the first one home.

"We're going to get a call today," Andi said confidently. "I know it."

*  *  *

*Andi was standing on a doorstep, handing over a plump tabby cat to a very grateful woman.*

*"Where would I have been without the Pet Finders Club?" the lady gasped with tears in her eyes. "I don't know how to thank you. I thought I'd never see Stripes again. You've made me so happy!"*

"Andi? Earth to Andi?"

A burst of laughter filled the classroom, and Andi opened her eyes with a jump. Mr. Dixon, her art and science teacher, was staring at her with a look on his face that said he was used to this.

Andi turned bright red. "Sorry, Mr. Dixon. I was miles away."

Natalie leaned over from the next table. "What were you thinking?"

"I was thinking about our club," Andi confessed, "and about how we're going to help the people of Orchard Park."

"Don't get ahead of yourself," Natalie warned. "We haven't had any calls yet. Besides, don't you think you've got more important things to worry about this morning?"

Andi looked at her in surprise. "Like what?"

Natalie rolled her eyes. "Like our spelling test in English?"

"We've got a *test*?" Andi gasped.

Natalie shook her head in mock despair. "And you think you're going to be able to find missing pets? You're losing it, girlfriend."

Tristan was waiting for them when they got out of school that afternoon. Natalie wasted no time telling him about Andi's outburst in homeroom.

"Nice job!" Tristan laughed as they walked out of the schoolyard and down the street.

"You may mock me," Andi said, wagging her finger at Tristan, "but someone has to think about what's going to happen when the calls start coming in."

She glanced over at Natalie, who was fiddling with something small and shiny. "What's that?" she asked, forgetting about the Pet Finders Club for a moment.

Natalie looked up. "My new cell phone," she said, holding it up. "I told my mom I would text message her after school and let her know what I was doing."

"Why didn't you just tell her this morning that you'd be with us?" asked Tristan. "By the way, Dean's making his famous tuna pasta, if you want to stay over for supper." Tristan's parents worked evenings and weekends running their real estate business, so Tristan's thirteen-year-old brother Dean usually did the cooking.

"Anything Dean cooks would be fine by Natalie," Andi teased. "Tuna pasta, beans on toast, deep-fried worms . . . Right, Nat?"

Natalie blushed furiously. "It's more fun sending a text," she said, ignoring Andi's comment.

"You should talk, Andi," Tristan said slyly. "Nat isn't Dean's only admirer, is she?"

Andi laughed. "I really like your brother," she said, "and he's pretty cute, but no way would I eat fried worms for the guy."

"Here, what do you think?" said Natalie, handing over the tiny silver cell phone.

Trying not to look impressed, Tristan turned it over. "Hey, it's got a hole in the back," he said.

"It's supposed to, wise guy!" Natalie protested. "You take pictures with it, and then you can send them to your friends."

Andi looked doubtful. "My cell phone doesn't take pictures," she pointed out.

"Neither does mine," said Tristan. "So, who exactly are you going to send all these pictures to? Sounds like a waste of money to me."

Andi giggled. "He's got a point, Nat."

Natalie snatched the phone back. "My mom thinks it's great, and she knows about stuff like this. You'll just

have to update to the twenty-first century, both of you,"
she said crossly. "Everyone's going to have one of these
someday."

"Actually, it could be useful for the Pet Finders Club,"
Andi said, seeing that Natalie was getting upset. Natalie's mom and stepdad were quite wealthy, so Nat had
lots of stuff other kids at school didn't, like a big house
with a pool. Sometimes Natalie got a bit self-conscious
about it and worried that people only wanted to be her
friend because they thought she had a flashy lifestyle.
"People could send pictures of their lost pets to us,"
Andi went on, warming to the idea. "Hey, maybe we
could call everyone who left messages today to ask
them if they've got any cell phone pictures of their pets!
That would really help, don't you think?"

"You're obsessed!" Natalie cried, shoving the cell
phone into her backpack. "It's only Monday. I bet you
there won't be any messages at all."

"You are so wrong," Andi replied breezily. "I'm telling
you, the Pet Finders Club is going to be so busy that we
won't know which pet to look for first."

Suddenly bubbling over with enthusiasm for the project, she yanked her backpack higher on her shoulder
and took off running. Back in Florida, Andi had run
a lot, not just for fun, but for the track team at her

school. She ran the whole way home, enjoying the feeling of her sneakers pounding against the sidewalk. She loved keeping fit — so fit that Tristan and Natalie had trouble keeping up. She didn't stop to wait for them, but kept going all the way to Aspen Drive, leaping up the steps to the front porch three at a time and shoving her key in the lock before she had stopped moving.

"Hey, Buddy!" Andi called as she burst through the front door, tickling the ecstatic Jack Russell behind his soft brown ears. "Did the phone ring all day and drive you crazy?"

"I don't think so, Andi," puffed Natalie, coming up behind her and peering at the phone. "There aren't any messages."

"What? No messages at all?" Andi wailed. "Not even one?"

Natalie shook her head.

Andi checked the pad by the phone, in case her mom had written down any messages at lunchtime. But there was nothing. Then she lifted up the phone to check that it was working. The dial tone buzzed in her ear, same as usual. She groaned with disappointment and sat down at the bottom of the staircase. Buddy stretched up to lick her face.

"Were there any messages on your cell phone?" Natalie asked.

Andi shook her head. "I checked about a hundred times today."

Tristan struck a Scarlett O'Hara pose, flinging his arm across his foreheard and hanging off the banister. "Cheer up," he said, jumping down. "'After all, tomorrow is another day!'"

Andi laughed, feeling a little better. *Maybe he's right,* she thought. *Maybe someone will call tomorrow. And at least no one's feeling sad and lonely about any lost pets tonight.*

But no one called the next day, or the day after that. Somehow, Andi managed to concentrate in class and only check her cell at lunch, and by Thursday, she'd stopped running straight home to check for messages.

"I can't believe it," she sighed on Friday afternoon, as she sat on one of the swings in the park. Natalie and Tristan swung gently beside her, watching Buddy and Jet, Natalie's gorgeous black Labrador, playing tug of war with a piece of old rope. "This whole project's looking like a total waste of time."

"I guess everyone in Orchard Park looks after their pets too well," Natalie remarked. She leaned back in the

swing to stare at the sky. "They need to be more careless, like we were with our dogs," she said sarcastically.

"And like my family was with Lucy," Tristan said gloomily. Lucy was the name of his cat, who had disappeared several months ago and never turned up. Andi knew that Tris was beginning to think he'd never see her again.

Natalie looked uncomfortable. "Sorry, Tristan! I didn't mean that about being careless. It was just a joke."

"No joke," said Tristan bitterly. "Just the cold, hard truth." He pushed on his swing and flew up in the air, almost coming off the seat.

"Cats are different than dogs," said Andi. "They're more independent. No one ever knows where a cat is twenty-four hours a day."

"Except the cat," Natalie quipped.

Tristan gave a half-smile. "I know," he said. "I just miss her. I don't know what's worse, thinking something awful's happened or thinking she prefers living with someone else."

"So, what are we going to do about the Pet Finders Club?" Andi prompted.

Tristan shrugged. "Maybe we'll have to start kidnapping a few animals, just to get the ball rolling," he joked.

"It'll happen, Andi," Natalie said comfortingly. "Maybe

people lose their pets over the weekend. You know, when they take their dogs out. It's Saturday tomorrow."

Andi tried hard to think positively as she let herself in the front door. But she couldn't help glancing at the phone as she hung up her fleece. A big fat zero blinked back at her. She plodded into the kitchen to give Buddy his dinner, and then plodded into the living room, where she collapsed on the couch with a sigh.

"Cheer up, Andi," said her mom, looking up from some spreadsheets that she had brought home to work on. "Sighing isn't going to make the phone ring."

"I know I shouldn't feel so down, but I can't help it," Andi said miserably.

Judy Talbot stacked her papers neatly together and came over to give Andi a hug. "I think you should go to bed and get a good night's rest," she said. "Tomorrow's another day, right?"

*Tomorrow*, thought Andi as she made her way up the stairs with Buddy glued to her heels. *Always tomorrow.*

Saturday morning was bright and clear. Pulling on her favorite sweatshirt and jeans, Andi padded downstairs to find some breakfast. She smelled pancakes as she came into the kitchen.

"Morning." Her mom smiled, piling hot pancakes onto

a plate. "Maple syrup is on the table, and there are fresh strawberries. I'm doing banana and blueberry smoothies, too."

Andi's mouth watered. "This is great, Mom," she said. "What's the occasion?"

Mrs. Talbot smiled. "I just thought breakfast together would be nice," she said. "We haven't done it in a while, have we?"

Andi thought about the breakfasts she and her mom used to have out on the deck in Florida. It seemed like a hundred years ago. There was no chance of eating outside now, with a cold gray October sky hanging over the backyard. Andi watched her mom switch on the blender, swirling the bananas and blueberries together until the mixture was a beautiful shade of violet.

"I'm not going to worry about the Pet Finders Club today," Andi declared, helping herself to a pancake and topping it with two fat strawberries.

"Glad to hear it," said her mom, pouring out the smoothies and sitting down opposite her. "How about we head out of town for the day and do a little exploring? There must be some great places we could take Buddy."

Andi was about to say it was a brilliant idea — especially because they still hadn't had a chance to see the

mountains that temptingly peeped over the horizon —
when the phone rang. Mrs. Talbot reached over to pick
up the receiver.

"Hello? Christine?" her mom sat up straight in her
chair. "Slow down, what's the matter?"

Andi held her forkful of pancake in midair. Was that
Christine Wilson from Paws for Thought? What was going on?

Mrs. Talbot listened intently. "Well, at least the police
got there quickly," she said. "I'll bring Andi over right
away. I'm sure she'll want to be there."

She put the receiver down and stared at Andi. "Paws
for Thought has been robbed!"

"Robbed?" Andi echoed in disbelief. "What was
stolen?"

Andi's mom shook her head. "Pretty much everything," she said. "The animals, the feed. And they've
taken Max as well!"

# Chapter Four

As if in answer to Andi's prayers, all the traffic lights between her house and Paws for Thought were green. While Mrs. Talbot drove as fast as she safely could to Main Street, Andi clung tightly to Buddy and closed her eyes. She couldn't believe all the animals were gone. And Max! *Serves you right for wanting pets to disappear,* she thought bleakly. *Be careful what you wish for. It might come true.*

Mrs. Talbot swung into the tiny parking lot outside Paws for Thought and slammed on the brakes. Tristan and Natalie were standing on the sidewalk, waiting for Andi. They both looked grim.

"Have the police been here yet?" Andi asked breathlessly as her mom disappeared inside the store to talk to Christine. Buddy bounced around her feet, sensing the urgency in the air. "Do they have any idea who did it? How's Christine?"

"She's pretty bad," Natalie said, shaking her head.

"The police came right over and searched the place for evidence. They're coming back later to make a list of the missing animals," said Tristan. He made a face, his freckles standing out even more than usual against his pale skin. "Looks like the Pet Finders Club suddenly has a whole lot of pets to find. I feel . . . " He trailed off, looking more solemn than Andi had ever seen him. "I don't know what I feel," he said unhappily. "Guilty, maybe."

Andi squeezed his arm. "Me, too," she said. "I feel like I made this happen by wishing someone would lose their pet."

"This isn't our fault," Natalie told them sensibly. She flipped her hair over her shoulder — today it was in a ponytail with a silver seashell clip — and pushed open the door to the store. "This is our chance to help, right? So let's quit moaning and go make ourselves useful."

Mrs. Talbot came out of the store and overheard Natalie. "I agree, Christine really needs you guys today. Give me a call later to let me know how you're doing."

As her mom's car pulled away, Andi looked around Paws for Thought in dismay. It had been completely ransacked. The floor was covered with upended cages, and only the fish, the hamsters, a couple of rabbits, the chinchilla, and the guinea pigs were left. The snakes were gone and so was the little gray rabbit. There were no canaries and no lizards. The squashy pile of pet beds that usually stood in the window had been tipped over and scattered all over the floor. A turtle was making slow progress through heaps of spilled birdseed and a pile of dented dog food cans, and Buddy headed furtively toward a torn bag of dog treats in the corner. Andi could hardly believe it was the same place.

Christine was sitting on the stool behind the counter, her hands wrapped around a mug of coffee. She looked even paler than Tristan and her eyes were red. "Thanks for coming, guys," she sniffed. "I feel like this is all a dream, and when I wake up, Max will be under my feet, wanting his breakfast. Fisher's coming later. I feel like I need a lot of friendly faces around today."

"I'm sure Fisher will be a great help, Christine," Natalie said earnestly, scooping the turtle up out of harm's way. "He seems like the kind of guy who would be good in a crisis."

Andi bit back a smile. Only Natalie could play matchmaker at a time like this. Out on Main Street, a jackhammer started up. She raised her voice to be heard over the noise. "Max will turn up soon," she said. "Everyone knows him around here. You can't exactly disguise a golden cocker spaniel."

"You could dye his fur black," Tristan said thoughtfully.

Natalie glared at him. "That's so helpful — *not*."

Tristan glared back. "Never discount anything," he said. "Not until you're sure of your facts." He swung around to face the pet store owner. "Who do you know who might have robbed you, Christine?"

Christine blinked. "I'm sure I don't — "

"Do you have any enemies?" Tristan cut in, pacing back and forth. "Do you owe any money, or have you upset anyone recently?"

"*Upset* anyone?" Christine echoed, startled. "Not that I — "

"How is your security?" Tristan went on, sounding severe. "Do you have an alarm system? Do you — "

"*Tristan!*" Andi hissed.

Tristan turned to look at her. "I'm in the middle of some important questioning here," he said crossly.

"And you're not waiting to hear any answers!" Andi protested.

"Ah." Tristan blushed. "Good point. So, where was I?"

"You were going to get us some pretzels to eat so we

can think straight," Christine said firmly, pushing him toward the little kitchen at the back of the store.

"Is there any chance that Max could have wandered off last night?" Andi asked once Tristan was out of the way. "After all, he doesn't have a cage."

Christine shook her head. "I know he runs out of the store from time to time, but he always comes back. Last night, he was downstairs with the pets. It was a hot night, and he likes sleeping on the cool tiles down there."

"Didn't you hear anything during the night, or early this morning?" Natalie wondered. "If someone had broken in, wouldn't Max have barked?"

"I've been using earplugs because of all the construction work on Main Street," Christine admitted. "They start very early, and we've all been losing sleep." Her face clouded, and Andi thought she looked like she was going to cry. "But I'd much rather lose sleep than Max."

Tristan emerged from the kitchen with the pretzels. "We'll add them to our list of suspects!" he announced, sounding excited.

"Who?" said Natalie.

"The construction workers, of course," said Tristan.

Christine looked at him in surprise. "Why would they want to steal a store full of pets?"

"Who knows?" Tristan replied mysteriously, taking a bite out of his pretzel. "Maybe we need to find out."

Andi sighed. Tristan was a great friend, but he could be exhausting. "Listen, why don't we all check out the store and the backyard to see if there are any clues the police missed," she suggested.

"That's the first sensible suggestion we've had this morning," Natalie said.

"Just don't disturb anything," Christine warned. "The police are coming back again later."

"Okay," said Tristan, popping the last of his pretzel into his mouth and rubbing his hands. "We could ask some of the neighboring stores if they saw anything suspicious."

"Hey, a good idea at last!" Natalie exclaimed. "Slow down, Tristan, we don't want you burning out."

"You wait," Tristan grumbled. "I'm going to solve this crime single-handedly, and then you'll be sorry."

Tristan and Natalie took a look in the backyard while Andi and Christine walked around the store. Buddy sniffed in all the corners and wagged his tail a lot, but although Andi tried to encourage him to hunt for clues, all the little Jack Russell found was a dog chew covered in fluff and a rubber bone that had skidded under one of the shelving units.

Andi decided to join Natalie and Tristan in the yard. "Found anything yet?" she asked hopefully.

Natalie looked up from the pile of old crates she was hunting through and shook her head. "Nothing looks out of the ordinary," she confessed.

Andi frowned at Tristan. "How about you, Sherlock?"

Tristan was behaving very oddly. He was crouching next to Mrs. Harper's gate, sniffing at the hinges. "These have been freshly oiled," he said triumphantly.

Andi shrugged. "So? Mrs. Harper must have noticed the gate was squeaking. What's strange about that?"

Tristan lowered his voice. "Mrs. Harper has access to Main Street through Christine's yard. The fact that her gate has been oiled means she could have come into this yard last night *without making any noise*."

Andi opened her eyes wide. "Are you saying you think *Mrs. Harper* is the thief?"

"Shhhh!" Tristan hissed. "She might hear you!"

Andi peered over the gate into Mrs. Harper's yard. The small space contained nothing but a neatly stacked pile of crates and a couple of trash cans.

Natalie came over. She was taller than Andi, so it was easier for her to see into the yard. "I don't think Mrs. Harper's in today," she said, standing on tiptoe to get a better view. "Her drapes are closed, and I can't see a light in any of the upstairs windows."

"Mrs. Harper doesn't live above the store," Tristan informed them. "She has a house a few blocks away. But it's Saturday today. Everyone who owns a store comes in on the weekend. The fact that nobody's there is very suspicious, if you ask me."

Christine poked her head around the door into the yard. "Any extra clues out here?"

"Have you seen Mrs. Harper this morning, Christine?" Andi asked.

"No, why?"

Tristan shot a triumphant glance at Andi.

"No reason," said Andi. Mrs. Harper couldn't *really* be the thief, could she? It was true that she didn't like the pet store much, and she definitely didn't like Max. And, as Tristan said, the gate hinges had been oiled.

"Fisher will be here shortly to make a list of the missing animals for the police," said Christine. "It would really help if you started thinking about that. I used to keep better inventory sheets, but things have been so busy lately . . . " She trailed off, looking miserable.

"We'll start on it right away," Andi promised.

"Right after we've questioned a few of the local

stores," Tristan added, beckoning to Andi and Natalie to follow him down the alley that led to Main Street.

Mrs. Harper's store was called KnitWorld, and it stood to the left of Paws for Thought. There was a deli to the right, while a laundromat and a diner sat across the street.

With his great memory for names and faces, Tristan was quickly able to give the others some information about Paws for Thought's neighbors. "Amy Ling is the deli owner. She's friendly, though she doesn't speak much English. Elmer is the guy in the laundromat. You two find out if they saw anything, and I'll go and check out the diner."

He looked right and left and then ran across the road before Andi and Natalie could protest.

"Typical that he gets the diner!" Natalie grumbled. "Doesn't that boy ever stop eating?"

Andi clipped the leash on Buddy, who looked like he wanted to take himself off for a run. "If he gets some information, I don't care if he comes out with half the menu in his backpack! I'll go talk to Mrs. Ling, and you check with Elmer."

In the deli, Mrs. Ling was very polite, but it was clear that she hadn't seen anything useful. "Many people in

Main Street," she said, shaking her head. "Workers, you know? Difficult to say if they are strangers."

"I didn't have much luck either," said Natalie gloomily when Andi met her back outside Paws for Thought. "That Elmer guy just grunted at me. I guess he isn't too cheerful first thing in the morning."

Tristan came across the road then, holding three granola bars. "The waitress says she served five or six people this morning that she'd never seen before," he said, handing two of the bars to Andi and Natalie before wolfing down the third in two bites.

"That's great!" Andi exclaimed. "Did you get any descriptions?"

Tristan pulled a piece of paper out of his pocket. "There were five men and one woman," he read. "The men were all of medium height, with short brown or blond hair and dusty overalls."

"Construction workers," said Andi and Natalie together.

"And those descriptions cover pretty much anyone," Andi added. "Was the woman with one of the workers?"

"No," said Tristan, checking his notes. "She sat alone by the window with some kind of paperwork. She was wearing sunglasses, so the waitress didn't get a good look at her face."

"Sunglasses to do paperwork?" said Andi in surprise.

"I'll go back and see if that Elmer guy in the laundromat is awake yet," Natalie said thoughtfully. "The laundromat is right across a small alley from the diner, and the windows face each other. He could definitely have noticed the woman, especially if she was sitting right by the window."

"Why would he notice her and not the others?" Tristan objected.

"At that time of the morning, I'll bet she stood out if most of the people in the diner were construction men," said Natalie.

Andi and Tristan took turns scratching Buddy's tummy while Natalie ran back to the laundromat. It wasn't long before she returned, her eyes glowing in triumph.

"He remembers her!" she declared. "Dark hair, pale skin. He said she was looking at a set of drawings or something, but it was hard to see small details from where he was."

Her cell phone suddenly started ringing in a cute musical tune. Natalie rummaged through her bag, then rummaged again as the cell kept ringing.

"Having trouble finding it?" Tristan asked. "They should have supplied it with a magnifying glass, it's so small."

Natalie brought her head out of the bag. "You're only jealous," she snapped, before diving back again. "Ha!" She triumphantly pulled out the cell phone — just as it stopped ringing.

Before Tristan could say anything, a rasping metallic sound made them spin around. Very slowly, the metal shutters on the front of Mrs. Harper's store were cranking open.

"Hey!" Natalie exclaimed, forgetting about her cell. "Looks like KnitWorld is open for business after all."

Andi started over toward the craft store, but Tristan pulled her back. "Don't go over there yet!"

"But we need to question Mrs. Harper," Andi objected, trying to shake off Tristan's hand.

"Not until we have a few more facts," he insisted. "We can't let her see that we know anything." Andi decided not to point out that they *didn't* know anything, which was the problem. "Let's just wait a while," Tristan went on. "The police will be here soon. That should bring her around to find out what's going on, unless she wants to avoid the police for some reason."

Suddenly, an eerie quiet descended over Main Street. The jackhammer that had been pounding across the street had sputtered to a halt. Andi watched the workers gather around the open door of a white truck parked on the far side of the road. One guy was pouring cups of coffee and handing out donuts.

"Now we can think straight, without our brains rattling in our heads," said Tristan with relief. "What are the facts so far?"

"It looks like the real stumbling block is the fact that there are too many strangers in this part of town today," Natalie said with a sigh. "How are we supposed to get any information if the locals don't recognize half of their customers?"

Andi blinked. She'd just gotten a fantastic idea. "The locals may not recognize the customers," she said slowly, "but the customers would recognize each other."

"What do you mean?" Tristan asked.

"It's obvious!" said Andi. "All these strangers in town — they all seem to be construction workers, right?"

"Right," Tristan agreed, his face a mask of concentration.

"Except for the woman in the sunglasses," Natalie noticed.

Andi waved that fact away impatiently. "We'll come back to her later," she said. Then she pointed to the workers by the truck. "The workers all know each other, don't they? So wouldn't *they* recognize a stranger?"

# Chapter Five

There was a short silence as Tristan and Natalie figured out what Andi was saying. Then —

"Brilliant!"

"Great idea!"

They both started talking at once, with Buddy yapping to join in. Andi bent down to stroke his ears and quiet him.

"So," said Tristan. "Who's going over there to ask them?"

There were seven or eight workers standing together. They looked a little intimidating in their hard hats and reflective overalls, and Andi hesitated.

"Go on, Andi," Natalie said, prodding her. "It was your idea."

One of the workers was standing slightly apart from

the others. He looked a bit older, and Andi decided he must be the boss.

"Hurry up!" Tristan urged. "They're about to start work again."

Sure enough, the workers were putting their coffee mugs back in the truck and pulling on gloves. But Andi felt as if her legs were frozen to the sidewalk. Main Street suddenly seemed very wide.

At that moment, Buddy tugged free from his leash and bounded across the road.

"Buddy!" Andi ran across the road after him, her heart in her mouth in fear of a car coming out of no-where and hitting him. "Buddy, come here!"

Taking no notice, the Jack Russell headed straight for the construction workers and jumped up to shove his nose into the crumpled bag of donuts in the back of the truck.

Andi skidded to a halt beside the truck. "Buddy!" she scolded. "How many times have I told you about cross-ing roads without me?"

"Dogs only listen when they want to," said a laughing voice.

Andi turned around to see the older construction worker. "Tell me about it," she puffed, grabbing hold of

Buddy's collar and reattaching the leash. "'Walk' always seems to get Buddy's attention, but somehow 'come here' doesn't."

The man bent down and scratched Buddy's head. "I have a dog," he said. "A retriever. The kids love her."

Andi smiled as this man and some other construction workers gathered around to fuss over Buddy. He was a very useful member of the Pet Finders Club!

"Do you mind if I ask you a couple of questions, sir?" Andi asked the man.

"My name's Mick," he told her. "What do you want to know?"

Andi looked over at Natalie and Tristan, who grinned encouragingly and gave her the thumbs-up. She took a deep breath. "There was a robbery last night at Paws for Thought, the pet store across the street," she explained. "What time did you start work today?"

"Six o'clock," Mick replied. "We're usually the first, except for the guy who runs the diner. Why, do you suspect us?" The men laughed, but in a friendly way.

Andi felt her cheeks get hot. "Did you see any strangers acting suspiciously this morning, or maybe a vehicle you didn't recognize?"

Mick took off his hard hat and scratched his head. "Can't say as I did. Dave, Marlon — any of you fellas see a vehicle or a suspicious person on the road this morning?"

The other workers shook their heads. "Just the pet store lady's van," said one of them. "You know, that white one she drives."

"Hold on a second. Christine hasn't been out today," Andi said with a frown. "Are you sure it was her van? Did you see the logo on the side?"

The workman shrugged his shoulders. "I didn't notice any logo. But that dog of hers was staring out the back window, like he always does."

Andi stared at him. "You saw Max in the van? What time was that?"

"Is that the dog's name?" asked the worker. "I guess it was right when we arrived on-site."

"I don't suppose you got a license plate number or anything?" Andi pressed.

The worker shook his head. "I didn't see the license plate. Didn't see the driver either. Just the dog in a white van, like I said."

Andi felt like jumping for joy. It was a real clue! After thanking the workers, she raced across the road with Buddy, back to where Natalie and Tristan were standing. Then she told them, word for word, what the worker had said.

When Andi had finished talking, Natalie frowned.

"What's the matter?" Andi asked. "I thought you'd be pleased."

Natalie chewed her lip. "Aren't plain white vans just about the most common vehicle on the road?" she said. "Honestly, I don't see how that helps us at all."

"Oh." Andi suddenly felt miserable. Natalie sure knew how to cut to the chase. "You're right. It's nothing."

Natalie flushed. "I'm sorry. It's just — well, it's true. Isn't it?"

Tristan came to the rescue. "It may be true, but it's a start," he said firmly. "I think it's great, Andi. The only problem I can see with it is that Mrs. Harper doesn't drive a white van."

"So we can cross her off our suspect list?" Andi said hopefully.

"She could have rented one," Natalie pointed out.

Andi's heart sank again. "Great," she grumbled, scuffing the ground with her toe. Buddy sat close to her feet and leaned comfortingly against her legs.

Tristan nudged her. "Look across the street!" he hissed.

Andi looked up to see a dark-haired woman hurrying down Main Street. She was holding a stack of papers that fluttered and flapped in the wind, and a large pair of dark glasses were perched on the end of her nose. As they watched, a single piece of paper floated out of her grasp and wafted across the street toward them. The woman didn't seem to notice.

Sprinting down the street, Andi flung herself after the paper and grabbed it just before it blew out of her reach. Then she sauntered back to the others. "You wanted a clue?" she said with a grin, showing them the paper. "How's this?"

"Shouldn't we return it?" Natalie asked, looking nervously down the street after the woman. "It could be important."

"All the more reason to hold on to it," Tristan decided. He tapped the paper. "Take a look at this, guys. Suspicious, or what?"

The paper showed a map of Main Street with the names of all the stores neatly pencilled in. And right outside Paws for Thought, there was a large red cross.

Before they could figure out what the map might mean, a police car pulled up alongside them. Andi quickly pocketed the map as Tristan rushed over to the car and knocked on the window.

"Officer?" he said importantly when the policewoman behind the wheel rolled down the window. "My name is Tristan Saunders. Are you here about the robbery?"

The officer raised her eyebrows. "Yes, why? Do you know something about it?"

Tristan was stopped from answering by Christine, who came out of the store to greet the police officers. Andi felt a stab of pain at the sight of Christine's tear-stained face. She thought about poor Max and the other animals as she followed the police officers up to Christine's apartment, and almost felt like crying herself. In all her wishing for lost pets, she never thought the Pet Finders Club would get a case as sad as this!

The sight of Christine's warm, welcoming apartment cheered her up a little. It was neatly laid out, with two small bedrooms and a bright red living room. The sunflower-yellow kitchen was at the back, with an old pine table in the middle of its black-and-white checked floor.

Fisher Pearce was sitting at the table with a large pad of paper. He introduced himself to the police officers, who knew him already from his ASPCA work, and smiled at Andi and her friends. "You guys couldn't have started the Pet Finders Club at a better time," he said. "We need all the help we can get on this one."

After a quick explanation about the Pet Finders Club for the benefit of the police officers, Christine poured juice or coffee for everyone, and they settled down to list all the missing animals. Max was the only dog, as Christine preferred to leave puppies and kittens to professional breeders. But the list was still very long. Andi's heart sank down to the toes of her sneakers. How were they going to find one single tiny animal, let alone all of them?

"One macaw, one gerbil," read out one of the officers, "one rabbit, four snakes, three geckos, two monitor lizards."

"Those two had been ordered for Mr. Scarpetti," added Christine. "He's one of my best customers for reptiles. They were pretty valuable, I'm afraid."

"Two parakeets, two mice . . . "

"They'd just had babies," Natalie explained. "Six of them."

"Right. Eight mice, two canaries, and one golden cocker spaniel who answers to the name of Max," the officer finished. He raised his eyebrows. "Is that it?"

Everyone nodded.

"We've been looking around this morning, and Andi's got a clue for you," Tristan added.

Andi tried to kick him under the table. She wasn't about to tell the police about the paper — she had a nasty feeling that they should have given it straight back to the woman with the sunglasses — and she didn't want to hear all over again how useless her clue about the white van was. But the police officers were looking expectantly at her, so she told them about the van.

To her delight, the officers wrote it down. "Good work, Andi," said the female officer. "We can check our system for white van owners and ask around the local rental companies to see who may have reserved a van for the night."

"And we've got a suspect — ow!" Tristan yelped.

This time, Andi's kick had found its target. No way should they start accusing people — yet. Not until they had some real proof. "Do you think you'll find the animals? Even Max?" she asked loudly, trying to divert attention from Tristan.

Christine was twisting Max's plaid leash in her hands. "It's so strange not having him under my feet," she sniffed.

"Nice one, Andi," Tristan muttered, rubbing his shin under the table as Fisher handed Christine a tissue.

Feeling awful for making Christine cry, Andi made a silent promise to work *extra* hard on this case. She looked down at Buddy, sleeping peacefully between her feet, and remembered again how terrible she had felt when she lost him. She wouldn't wish that on her worst enemy, let alone someone who was her friend.

They headed back down to the store when the police officers asked to speak to Christine alone. Tristan immediately wanted another look at the map.

"Why didn't you tell the police about this, Andi?" Natalie asked curiously. "It's our best clue. Much better than the white van."

"We don't know what it is," Andi said. "It might not have anything to do with the robbery. Unlike the van."

"I want to look at it at home," said Tristan, folding the paper and putting it in his pocket. "There might be some real estate documents in our office that could help me figure the 'X' out."

"I think we should search the whole block for more clues," Andi suggested. "We've only looked in the backyard and the stores across the street so far."

"We didn't check the alley behind the yard," Natalie said. "That's definitely worth a look. It goes all along the block."

"And it's not just clues we should be looking out for," said Tristan as they headed outside. "Some of the animals may have gotten loose during the robbery. There are twenty-five on the list, including Max and the baby mice. That's a lot of pets to keep under control, even if the thief wasn't alone."

"You might have something there," Andi agreed. She looked down at Buddy. "You hear that, Bud? Sharpen up your nose. It could come in handy."

"I hope none of the snakes escaped," Natalie muttered. She suddenly didn't look too excited about the idea of poking around the alley.

Buddy pulled hard on his leash as he sniffed around, poking his nose into odd piles of trash and leaves. Andi walked slowly, straining her ears for any strange sounds.

*"Aaaghhh!"*

Her heart nearly stopped at the sudden, bloodcurdling shriek from Mrs. Harper's yard.

Mrs. Harper was standing beside her trash can with her hands over her mouth. She was wearing a white shirt with a flower embroidered on the front, and her face was as pale as the fabric.

"Are you okay, Mrs. Harper?" Natalie called as she, Tristan, and Andi raced over to see what was happening.

"I — saw — " Mrs. Harper stammered, "a snake!" she managed at last. "A killer snake! There, behind the trash can!"

"I'll get Christine," said Natalie hurriedly. "Here, Andi,

let me take Buddy. We don't want him biting it and making it mad."

"Don't panic," Tristan ordered. "We've got to stay calm." He let himself into Mrs. Harper's yard and crouched down to peer into the darkness behind the trash can. "Okay, I can see it," he said, his voice sounding muffled. "Andi, pass me a box or something that I can put over it. Snakes like the dark. We'll keep it quiet until Christine comes."

Mrs. Harper handed Andi a cardboard box with trembling hands, and Andi passed it to Tristan. He squeezed even further behind the trash can and very slowly placed the box over the snake.

"Got it!" he said, backing out. "It won't hurt you, Mrs. Harper. It's just a little garter snake."

"I don't care what it is," said Mrs. Harper, standing back. "It's a snake and that's all I need to know. I can't stand them! Awful, slimy creatures!"

"But they're not slimy," Tristan argued. "They're sort of dry and scaly."

Mrs. Harper shuddered. "You aren't making this any better, young man," she said. "It escaped from the pet store, didn't it? I knew that store was bad news the minute it opened!"

"But it wasn't Christine's fault — " Andi began.

Mrs. Harper glared at her. "Of course it was," she said. "Why else would a snake be loose in my yard? Do you think someone was taking it for a walk?"

Andi opened her mouth to answer, but just then, Fisher strode into the alley, pulling on his snake-handling gloves. Natalie and Buddy followed at a safe distance.

"Good catch, Tristan," said Fisher, reaching into the cardboard box. He held the little blue-black reptile up for everyone to see. It didn't look too bothered by its adventure, to Andi's relief.

"One down, twenty-four to go," Fisher said grimly, putting the snake back into the box.

# Chapter Six

"Mrs. Harper looked like she was going to faint back there," Tristan remarked, picking up his banana and mango smoothie. "It took a while to convince her that we weren't talking about twenty-four more snakes."

Christine had sent them over to the Banana Beach Café for a break. She wasn't going to open the store today, but she had a lot to do with insurance forms and assessing the damage that had been done. Fisher was going to stay and help, and when Tristan offered to pitch in, too, Natalie nudged him with her elbow so hard that he nearly fell out of the front door. She was determined to see Fisher become Christine's knight in shining armor, without anyone else hanging around.

Unexpectedly for October, the sun had come out, so they were sitting at an outside table. Buddy lay under

Andi's chair with just his nose sticking out into the sunshine.

Natalie stirred her smoothie with her plastic straw. "You know this means Mrs. Harper can't be the thief, don't you?" she said. "Look at how scared she was of that little snake. I don't like them much either, but that is a *serious* phobia. I can't see her stealing a bunch of reptiles, however mad she was about Max barking. I think that street plan is our best clue so far. We should focus on that."

Tristan drained his smoothie in one gulp and sat back in the shade of the umbrella. "I'm not prepared to let Mrs. Harper off the hook just yet," he said. "She could have had an accomplice."

"Yeah, right," said Natalie. She rolled her eyes at Andi. "Isn't there anything more practical we can do right now?"

"There's always posters," Tristan suggested. "Especially if we used a picture of Max. Like Christine said, everyone knows him in Orchard Park."

Andi wasn't listening as Tristan and Natalie discussed their tactics. She hadn't touched her smoothie, but had spent the past ten minutes fiddling listlessly with her spoon. First Buddy, now Max. How come the first pets to disappear since she had come to Orchard Park were all animals that she knew? She'd wished so hard for a case to solve, but not one this close to home! *I'm a jinx on the Pet Finders Club,* she thought sadly. *There's no other explanation. I'll have to resign.*

Back at Andi's house later that day, Tristan and Natalie leaned over her shoulder to get a better look at the design on the computer screen.

"The lettering should be bigger," said Tristan, leaning so close that his nose was almost touching the monitor. "And can't you zoom in on Christine's picture of Max? He's kind of far away."

"You've spelled *thought* wrong too," Natalie added. "It's got a 'G' in it."

Andi pushed back her chair. "I can't concentrate on this," she snapped. "You do it, Tristan. I'm going downstairs."

Tristan raised his eyebrows at Natalie as Andi stomped out of the room with Buddy close at her heels.

"What's up, Andi?" said Natalie, following her down to the living room. "You haven't said two words since we left the Banana Beach."

Andi threw herself down on the couch and hauled

Buddy up next to her. "I think I'm bringing bad luck to the Pet Finders Club," she said. "Three pets have disappeared since I came to Orchard Park, Nat: Buddy, Jet, and now Max. They're all pets I know. That's a weird coincidence, don't you think?"

Natalie looked amazed. "Don't be stupid! Buddy got lost because he was in a new town, Jet got lost before I even knew you, and Max has been stolen. None of those things has anything to do with you."

Andi buried her nose in the top of Buddy's warm furry head. "I just don't think I'm very good at this. My clue about the white van was no help. I could never have handled Mrs. Harper's snake situation as smoothly as Tristan did. The two of you don't need me. You'll do much better on your own."

Natalie folded her arms and stared down at Andi. "So you're bailing on us, just like that?" she said accusingly.

"It's not bailing," Andi protested. "I really think — "

"Actually, Andi, that's just it," Natalie snapped. "You're just thinking about yourself."

Andi went red, and Natalie sat down on the couch beside her. "We really need you," she went on. "If you hadn't found that map, we'd be pretty short on clues right now. You're great at designing posters, and I know you really care about the animals. Look who Tristan calls whenever something comes up. He calls *you*, not me. Doesn't that tell you something?"

"Yeah," said Andi, managing a tiny smile. "It tells me that 'A' comes before 'N' in Tristan's phone book."

Right on cue, Tristan appeared in the living room doorway, waving a stack of posters. "I printed these out," he announced. "What are we going to do with them?"

Natalie hauled Andi off the couch. "We're going to post them around the neighborhood," she said, looking at Andi. "Right?"

Andi took a deep breath. "Right."

Natalie cheered and gave Andi a hug.

"What's going on?" asked Tristan.

Natalie waved her hand at him. "Girl stuff," she said, and Tristan looked like he didn't want to know anything more.

Outside, the sun was casting dancing shadows through the golden October leaves on the trees. Among the three of them, they covered all the blocks between Andi's house and Main Street in no time, leaving posters on every prominent tree they could find. By the time they reached Paws for Thought, there was only one poster left.

The pet store looked forlorn and empty, with a CLOSED sign hanging on the door.

"Christine?" Andi called, stepping into the store. "Fisher?"

Christine was sitting on the floor surrounded by empty cages. "Fisher got called away, and I was on my own," she said in an odd voice. "I looked around for Max . . ." She burst into tears and started to get up, looking like a straw man with badly stuffed, wobbly legs.

Andi and the others rushed over to help.

"Everything got to me after Fisher left," Christine sniffed, dusting down her jeans. "I'm sorry. It's all so awful. My business is ruined, and Max is gone. What am I going to do?"

"You've got to think positive!" Tristan urged her.

"And we're nowhere near giving up," said Andi, showing Christine the new poster. "See? We've posted them all over the neighborhood."

Christine gave a watery smile. "Thanks, guys. Max looks great."

"It's going to work," Andi insisted. "I know it is."

Natalie pinned the poster in the store window while Tristan got Christine a glass of water. Then they helped feed the remaining animals and swept up the spilled sawdust and straw.

"One more animal to feed," Christine said at last, producing the plastic tub. "Let's go see our escapee." Tristan put on his hopeful face, making Christine hold up her hands in defeat. "Okay, you can feed the snake just this once," she said, handing Tristan the box of food. "Since you found him."

"Cool!" breathed Tristan.

The store doorbell tinkled. Andi saw a woman hovering at the door. She looked familiar, but Andi couldn't place her at first.

"Hello?" she said hesitantly. "Are you open?"

"Not really," Christine admitted. "As you can see, there isn't much to sell. We had a robbery this morning."

"Oh, I'm so sorry to hear that!" the woman exclaimed. She maneuvered a child's stroller through the door, and Andi saw a little girl fast asleep with her thumb in her mouth.

Suddenly, Andi remembered where she'd seen them before. "You're Liam's mom, aren't you?" she said.

The woman looked surprised. "Why, yes, I'm Mrs. Noble. Do you know my son?"

"He came in last week," Andi explained. "He wanted to look at one of the rabbits. It's lucky he didn't come today."

Mrs. Noble went pale. "Don't tell me that little lop-eared rabbit was taken too?"

"I'm afraid so," Christine said sadly.

"Oh, no!" Liam's mom looked dismayed. "I was going to get it for Liam's birthday, as a surprise. What am I going to do now?"

Andi felt desperately sad. She'd seen how much Liam had wanted the little gray rabbit.

"I always told Liam that his sister was too young for a pet," Mrs. Noble went on. "But she's growing up fast, and I figured it wouldn't do any harm. . . . Oh, gosh! It's just as well I didn't tell Liam what I was planning. This would have broken his heart."

A nasty thought wormed its way into Andi's mind as she listened. *Liam had been crazy about that rabbit. . . .*

"I'll get your number and let you know if the rabbit turns up," Christine promised Mrs. Noble. When they were done, Christine held the door open for the woman and the stroller.

Andi tugged at Natalie's sleeve. Natalie looked at her with raised eyebrows. "Are you thinking what I'm thinking?"

"You think Liam might have done it?" Andi whispered.

"He's just a kid!" Tristan said, sounding shocked.

"A kid with a big thing for rabbits," Natalie reminded him.

"Rabbits, maybe, but he didn't say anything about wanting a bunch of mice, a couple of monitor lizards, and a macaw, as well," Tristan pointed out. "Why would he bother stealing them, too?"

"Maybe he stole all the other animals so no one would suspect him," Andi suggested, though she felt sick as she said it. "After all, we found the garter snake out back. Perhaps he let the other pets loose and just kept the rabbit."

Tristan wasn't convinced. "What about the van?" he asked. "You're not telling me an eight-year-old kid can drive."

"He could have an older brother or something," Natalie offered.

"Wouldn't Liam's mom notice if the rabbit turned up at his house?" Tristan went on. "And if the rabbit isn't at Liam's house where he can see it and play with it, what was the point of the robbery in the first place? He might as well have left the rabbit here. At least that way he could take a look at it sometimes."

Natalie didn't have an answer to that one, and neither did Andi. She knew it all sounded unlikely, but she couldn't forget the longing expression on Liam's face, nor how upset he had been after his mom told him he couldn't have a rabbit. But would a little eight-year-old kid really break into a store?

"It doesn't sound possible when you put it like that, Tristan," Natalie admitted. "But I think we should keep it in mind. If all the other animals turn up except for the rabbit, we might be on to something. That's all I'm saying."

"Hey!" said Tristan, smacking his forehead. "I forgot to tell you about the map! I saw some architectural layouts on my dad's desk last night, for a new building the city's planning. The map we found looks just like them! I think it might have been designed on the same computer program that the city council uses."

The girls looked unconvinced.

"Are you sure?" asked Natalie. "How do we know that program isn't used by every designer?"

"Trust me," said Tristan. "These layouts used the same color ink and even some of the same markings for things like trees and fire hydrants."

"This case is beginning to get me down," Natalie sighed. "There are too many maybes. We'd better get a serious lead soon or my brain will explode."

Suddenly, Buddy stiffened and let out a loud yap.

"What is it, boy?" said Andi.

Buddy barked again, then whined excitedly. This time, an answering bark came back, just audible above the noise from the street.

"Is that who I think it is?" said Natalie, her eyes opening wide. A very weary, very dirty golden cocker spaniel was standing outside the front window.

"It's Max!" Andi shouted, rushing to open the door. "Look, he's come back!" Max took one look at Andi and threw himself at her, barking and yelping and wagging his tail so hard that it was almost a blur.

Christine emerged from the storeroom at Olympic speed. "Max!" She knelt down as the dog tried to lick every part of her at the same time. "Look at you! Where have you been?"

Tristan managed to catch one of Max's paws as the dog squirmed on the dusty ground. "His pads are pretty sore," he remarked. "From the look of it, he's come a long way."

Christine planted a kiss on the end of the spaniel's nose, and laughed as he tried to lick her chin. "You need a bath, old boy," she said. "Come on, let's get you cleaned up. Then, to prove how much I've missed you, you can have steak for your dinner!"

Andi, Tristan, and Natalie joined in with the messy

business of bathing the dog. After some damp struggles, Max submitted to the scrubbing with good grace, though he kept turning around to lick Christine. Buddy retreated to a safe corner of the bathroom, away from the splashing water.

They had just lifted Max out when there was a knock at the back door. It was Mrs. Harper, carrying a large pot, full of what smelled like chicken casserole.

"Is that for us?" Christine said with surprise. "You didn't need to do that, Mrs. Harper."

Her neighbor set the casserole down on the kitchen table. "This is a thank you for dealing with that snake this morning," she said with a smile. "And an apology for not realizing you'd had a robbery. I'm so sorry, dear." She looked down at Max, who was sniffing around her feet. "And I see that your dog is back," she added, sounding genuinely pleased. "That's good. I know I'm not much of an animal person, but it must have been terrible when he disappeared."

"It was," Christine agreed. "I can't tell you how relieved I am to have him back — even though I still want to know where all the other animals are."

"That's that," Tristan whispered to Andi and Natalie. "Mrs. Harper's no thief."

"Why are you so certain all of a sudden?" Andi asked.

"Back at the Banana Beach, she was still your primary suspect!"

Tristan grinned. "That casserole smells too good," he said. "No way can thieves cook like that! Hey, do you think Christine will ask us to stay for dinner?"

Natalie rolled her eyes. "Don't you think we've got more important things to worry about, like figuring out how Max got back?"

Andi glanced down at Max, who was sprawled on the floor, panting. *Where have you been?* she wondered. *And where are the others?* They were no closer to solving the robbery than they'd been before Max came back. It wasn't the first time that Andi wished — more than anything — that animals could talk!

# Chapter Seven

Early on Sunday morning, Andi snuggled deeper under her quilt while Buddy tried to lick her nose.

"You can have your breakfast in a minute, Bud!" she protested. Suddenly, the pet store robbery flew into her mind. Max may have come back, but there were still twenty-three missing pets that could be in danger.

Buddy barked as Andi sat up and flung back the quilt. "You'd better be good today," she told him. "I'm going to need your nose to track down all those pets."

After a quick shower, she pulled on stretch running pants and a long-sleeved T-shirt. *If we meet that thief today, he's going to have to run pretty fast to get away from me*, she told her reflection as she pulled a cap over her shoulder-length brown hair.

Her mom was on the phone. Looking up as Andi approached, Mrs. Talbot smiled. "Yes, I've got that," she said, cradling the receiver under her chin. "1258 Ash Grove. Thank you, Mr. Edwards. Someone will be over right away."

"Who was that?" Andi asked eagerly.

"The Pet Finders Club has had a call," her mom announced. "A man called Mr. Edwards saw your poster on Ash Grove. He has some baby mice in his garden and wondered if any were missing from the pet store."

"There *were* some baby mice," Andi gasped. "Wow, our first call!"

"You can tell the others after breakfast," Mrs. Talbot told her. "If you're going to be finding pets all day, first you need some food inside you."

Andi had never finished her toast and orange juice so fast. Then she piled some food in a bowl for Buddy and let him outside for a quick morning run before heading back to the phone to call Tristan and Natalie.

"Ash Grove?" Tristan said, sounding excited. "That's not too far from Main Street. They could definitely be Christine's mice. See you there in ten minutes!" Natalie also promised to get there as quickly as she could.

Andi stuffed an apple into her jacket pocket for later, gave Buddy a dog treat to make up for not taking him, and set off at a jog in the direction of Ash Grove. Even without doing a proper warm-up, she covered the sidewalk at a smooth, speedy pace. At this rate, her soccer coach would be amazed at how fit she was getting!

When she got there, Natalie was just being dropped off by her mom, Mrs. Peters, in her big, gold Jeep. Tristan came tearing around the corner on his skateboard a few minutes later.

"Cross your fingers," Andi said to the others as she pushed the bell.

A tall man in dark-rimmed glasses opened the door. "Hey, you were quick!"

"The Pet Finders Club is always ready for action, sir," said Tristan.

"So I see," Mr. Edwards smiled. "The mice are in the backyard. I didn't get too close, in case I frightened them."

When they reached the yard, Mr. Edwards pointed to a small hole at the bottom of the wooden fence. Andi knelt down and got as close to the hole as she dared. Then she took a look inside. Four pairs of tiny bright eyes looked back at her.

"Well?" Tristan asked hopefully.

She sat back on her heels with a sigh and shook her head. "I think these little guys are wild mice," she said. "Very cute, but not the ones we're looking for." The first thing she'd noticed was that the mice were brown.

Christine's mice were white, with ruby-red eyes. It was the wrong family.

The Pet Finders Club tried not to look too disappointed as Mr. Edwards apologized for the mistake. He seemed quite alarmed that he had discovered a possible rodent infestation, rather than some cherished pets.

"Why don't you come back to my house?" Andi suggested as they walked away. "My numbers are on the poster. Someone else might have called."

"Do you have any food?" Tristan asked. "I didn't eat any breakfast. I need fattening up here."

Andi laughed. For a kid who ate a lot, Tristan was remarkably skinny. "Sure we do," she said. "Just leave some for us, okay?"

They sat in Andi's backyard while they waited for the phone to ring, Natalie filing her nails and Tristan crunching his way through an apple. Andi leaned her head back and closed her eyes, soaking up the sun. It wasn't as hot as in Florida, but it was just as welcome.

As soon as the phone rang, Andi was on her feet and running inside to pick it up.

"Hello?" she said breathlessly into the receiver.

"Is this the Pet Finders Club?" said a voice with a strong European accent. "I have a macaw in my laundry room. Could you come take a look?"

Andi jotted down details of the address. It was on the other side of town, but it sounded promising. Andi's mom agreed to let them go on their own when they promised to call if they needed anything, and, after a quick call to Christine, the Pet Finders Club jumped on a bus to check out their latest lead.

Half an hour later, they found themselves in a huge, wild yard, with a man who introduced himself as Mr. Lipinski. He had a shock of pure white hair, and he was wearing his hand-knitted sweater inside out. Leading them around the back of the house, he threw open his laundry room door with a flourish. Sitting on top of the washing machine and preening its glossy blue-and-yellow feathers was a long-tailed macaw. It looked up as Andi and the others peered inside, clacked its beak, and then returned to its preening.

"It certainly looks like the one from Paws for Thought," said Natalie. "It's the right color and everything."

Andi agreed, but Tristan didn't look so sure. "I don't remember Christine's macaw having that bump on its beak," he said.

Mr. Lipinski snorted in disbelief. "It is yours!" he insisted. "Wild macaws in Seattle? Impossible!"

The bird cawed and flapped its wings, nearly knocking over a box of detergent on a nearby shelf. Then, oddly, Andi heard a very similar birdcall — from somewhere outside the house.

"Did you hear that?" she said, turning to the others. "That sounded like another macaw."

Mr. Lipinski's eyes widened. "I have two macaws now?"

Andi headed outside with the others close behind. They followed the sound of rustling wings and chirping birds down to the end of the yard, beyond Mr. Lipinski's fence. It was difficult to see through the trees screening Mr. Lipinski from his neighbors, but Andi thought she could make out the edge of a large, wire-mesh cage.

"Do your neighbors keep birds, Mr. Lipinski?" she asked.

The macaw in the laundry room screeched, drowning out Mr. Lipinski's answer. Immediately, the air was filled with a madly fluttering response from the wire cage next door.

"That's not just a couple of birds," Tristan whispered to Andi. "That's an entire aviary!"

Mr. Lipinski looked very surprised when Andi pointed out the super-sized birdcage. "You think maybe my macaw comes from there?"

"Well, yes," Andi said patiently, wondering how on

earth Mr. Lipinski hadn't realized that the racket at the end of his yard was an aviary. "Perhaps we'd better ask if they've lost any of their birds."

Tristan captured the bird by offering it a piece of apple. It was quite tame and appeared to be well cared for, though on closer inspection they could all see that it wasn't the one from Paws for Thought.

Mr. Lipinski thanked them profusely as he showed them to the gate. "An aviary!" he kept saying. "At the back of my yard!"

"Did you notice how his sweater was inside out?" Natalie giggled as they made their way next door with the macaw held firmly under Tristan's arm.

"Maybe he's a mad scientist?" Tristan suggested.

"He's just a little eccentric," Andi protested. "There's nothing wrong with that."

The macaw had indeed come from the aviary next door, and the owners were extremely grateful for its return. But the Pet Finders Club were no closer to finding any more of Christine's missing pets. It was beginning to look as if they had vanished into thin air.

The kids walked slowly back to the bus stop, down a street full of shiny new office buildings. Andi checked the timetable. The next bus wasn't due for another ten minutes. Settling down on the bench in the bus shelter,

Andi took a look at the buildings around her. One of them had four graceful pillars and a clock tower.

"Is that City Hall?" she asked the others curiously.

Tristan shrugged. "Sure. Government buildings look the same all over, right?"

"City Hall?" Andi echoed as something fell into place with a satisfying clunk. "As in, the place where we suspect the lady with sunglasses works?"

They all jumped to their feet as if the bench was scalding hot.

"I don't believe it," Natalie said faintly, pointing at the wide sloping steps outside City Hall. "Look who's coming!"

The dark-haired woman had her sunglasses placed firmly on the top of her head, but Andi recognized her immediately. She was deep in conversation with a blond man in a dark suit.

"She'd better look up in a minute," Tristan observed. "Or else she's going to walk straight into that pile of — "

"Ugh!" Andi and Natalie wrinkled their noses as the dark-haired lady looked down at the mess on her shoe.

"You know something?" they heard her say to her colleague. "I really, really *hate* dogs."

Tristan could barely contain himself. "She's practically confessed!" he whispered to the others. "She hates animals, and she's got a street plan with a big red cross outside the pet store. We should go and confront her right now!"

The bus pulled up with a squeal of hydraulic brakes. "Not now, Tristan," Andi said firmly, pushing him up the steps. "We know who she is and where she works, right? We can't go up and confront her, not without a few more facts."

But as the bus pulled away and Andi stared out of the window at City Hall, she couldn't help wondering if maybe they should have followed her after all.

There were no more calls for the Pet Finders Club on Monday. On Tuesday, after school, Andi and the others went to the Banana Beach Café to talk about Plan B. Or was it Plan C? Andi had lost count. She was starting to lose sleep about the whole case, too. The police hadn't found anything yet, and Christine was getting more and more anxious about her business. They all agreed not to worry her about the strange street plan just yet. It was clear that the only thing Christine could think about right now was whether her pets were safe and well. It was all so frustrating.

Jango Pearce came over and put three banana-and-pecan muffins on the table.

"We didn't order these," Natalie told him.

"On the house," said Jango with a smile. "You look like you need cheering up."

"I just cheered up," Tristan declared, reaching for a muffin. "Thanks, Mr. Pearce."

"Bananas!" squawked Long John Silver, the Banana Beach parrot, eyeing the muffins with interest. "More bananas!"

"Fisher's got a little good news for you," Jango said, and tapped his nose.

"We need all the good news we can get," Andi sighed. "What is it?"

"You can ask him yourself," Jango said, nodding toward the door. Fisher was hanging his coat on a peg.

It certainly was good news. "Christine just found the canaries," Fisher announced. "They were all sitting on the fence behind the store this afternoon. Seems like they took a holiday, then decided to come home for some birdseed."

"Great!" Andi cheered and high-fived Tristan and Natalie.

"Bananas! More bananas!" screeched Long John Silver.

*Craaaa!*

"Hey!" Andi swung around and stared out of the

Banana Beach window. "That wasn't Long John Silver."

"Look!" Natalie jumped to her feet and pointed. There, sitting on the telephone wire above Main Street, was a blue-and-yellow macaw!

"Mr. Pearce?" Tristan said. "Please tell me there are no aviaries around here."

"Apart from in here?" Jango joked, glancing at his parrot. "No."

Feeling like she was turning into something of a bird expert, Andi coaxed the macaw down from the wire with a chunk of muffin. Inside, Long John Silver waddled up and down the bar, cracking his beak in excitement at the sight of the strange macaw through the window. Buddy barked jealously and tried to nip at the feathers in the macaw's tail.

Natalie pulled out her cell phone. "I have to take a photo of this," she announced. "I'll e-mail it to you both."

"Great phone," Fisher commented, as Andi and Tristan stood next to each other with the macaw. "I've got the same model."

"Really?" Natalie said. "That's so cool! I'll be able to send you the picture, too."

"Whoop-de-doo," said Tristan, making a face. "Come on, let's take this feathered guy back to Christine before Long John Silver falls in love."

The blue-and-green parrot opened his beak in a yawn, to show Tristan exactly what he thought of that remark.

Finding the macaw was the start of a great streak of pet-finding — although Andi had to admit it was more luck than detective work. After school on Wednesday, Tristan came running into Paws for Thought to say that he'd seen the parakeets sitting side by side in a tree behind the diner. They tempted the little blue birds down from the branches with handfuls of sunflower seeds, and the pair were soon safely back inside their cage. Max had returned to his customary spot in the store window, and watched all the activity with great interest.

Then the most exciting discovery so far was made. Mick the construction worker came in, cradling an old jacket in his arms like a newborn baby. Nestled in the folds of the jacket was the gray lop-eared rabbit, curled up and fast asleep.

"I recognized her from your store window," Mick explained quietly. "I didn't want to wake her — she looked so comfortable. Whoever left this jacket in the doorway sure did this little lady a favor. Say, is she for sale? My kids would love her."

"I think she's reserved," said Andi.

Christine looked surprised. "She is? I've been in such a muddle since the robbery. Are you sure?"

"You remember Mrs. Noble?" said Andi. "She wanted her as a surprise for Liam's birthday. You took her number."

"There goes another suspect," Tristan sighed, as Christine thanked Mick and took him to look at the chinchilla instead.

"Yep," said Andi with satisfaction, putting the rabbit back in her cage and sticking a RESERVED sign on the bars. "Isn't it great? My hunch about Liam was totally and utterly wrong."

"Some detective you are," Tristan grunted.

Andi punched him gently on the arm. "Hey, I'm the one who found the street plan and recognized City Hall," she said. "We may be running out of suspects now that Liam's out of the picture, but that's good, right? The fewer suspects we have, the closer we are to finding out the truth!"

# Chapter Eight

Christine smiled broadly as she came over to Andi and the others.

"That construction worker just bought the chinchilla for his kids," she announced. "Not only are you guys finding my pets, you're bringing in customers, too! I think we all deserve a break, don't you? Chocolate-chip cookies upstairs."

*It's great to see Christine looking so positive again*, Andi thought happily, taking the stairs two at a time, *and I helped make that happen.* The thought put an extra bounce in her step as she jumped up the last three stairs and into Christine's apartment.

"How many pets are still missing?" Natalie asked as she sat down at the table.

Andi counted on her fingers. "The mice, the gerbil, the snakes, and the lizards."

"Didn't Christine say the lizards were the most valuable animals in the store?" said Natalie.

"Yes." Andi sighed. "Typical, isn't it?"

Christine poured milk for everyone, and they sat around her kitchen table eating the cookies. Max lay with his head on Christine's feet, giving the occasional snore, while Buddy propped his nose on Andi's knee and watched her hopefully as she ate. Suddenly, Natalie's cell phone let out the shrill cry that meant she had a text message. Tristan jumped so far that he knocked over his glass of milk. Max leaped up indignantly as it splashed onto his head.

Andi stood up and reached into a cabinet for some paper towels — and nearly fell over backward when she saw a pair of bright beady eyes staring out at her.

"Hey!" she exclaimed. "There's something in here!"

Everyone abandoned the spilled milk and crowded around her to look. Andi peeped cautiously inside the cabinet again. It was a gerbil — and there was only one place it could have come from! It had found a box of mac-and-cheese, and by the look of its round stomach, it had been dining well for the past week. Andi reached in and gently picked it up.

"So, now there's just the mice and the reptiles to

find," she said when they went down to the store to put the gerbil back in its cage.

"The reptiles, huh?" said Tristan, fondling Max's ears. The cocker spaniel leaned adoringly against his leg. "Funny how the most valuable animals are still missing, don't you think?"

"Apart from the chinchilla," Natalie pointed out. "If the thief only wanted valuable animals, why did she get left behind?"

Tristan frowned, thinking hard. "It doesn't make sense," he said.

"I've been thinking about Max," Andi added, looking down at the golden spaniel. "Christine told us how he loves white vans," she reminded them. "You saw how he reacted to that birdseed delivery truck the other day! Isn't it possible that Max jumped in for fun, just for the ride?"

They stared at each other.

"That's a good point," said Natalie. "I wonder which pets our thief *meant* to take, and which ones escaped — or were freed — by accident."

"Hey, maybe I'm a decent detective after all!" Andi said triumphantly.

"Maybe," said Tristan. "But we've still got to find the thief. With Mrs. Harper and Liam out of the picture, we're down to the sunglasses lady. Do you think the red "X" on the map might have meant the city council wants Paws for Thought out of the way?"

"That's an idea!" Andi remarked. She was finally feeling her detective abilities come to life. "Maybe the thief took the most valuable animals, thinking Christine would have to shut down if she didn't make the money?"

"It still doesn't explain the chinchilla — unless the thief just didn't know about its value. But this could be huge," said Tristan. "What do you say we go stake out City Hall?"

"We should have followed the lady with the sunglasses when we had the chance," Natalie said, sounding glum.

"If it's really her, she won't get away," Andi replied. "The Pet Finders Club will see to that." She sounded more confident than she felt.

Andi was late meeting the others at the park the next afternoon. She'd had to run home to grab Buddy and check the messages there, first. They'd chosen to meet at a park at the other end of town, near City Hall.

"We'd almost given up on you," Tristan called from the swing he was on as Andi tugged Buddy away from an interesting smell on the path. "We've gotta get over to City Hall soon if we want to try and catch the woman in sunglasses coming out of work."

"Where's Nat?" she asked, taking a seat on a swing next to Tristan.

He pointed. "She's taking photos of Jet and Max with that cell phone of hers. Honestly, what's the point? The photos come out really small and grainy, and there's only about three other people on the planet who can receive them."

"You're just jealous," Andi teased, watching Natalie try to get a shot of the wriggling dogs as Buddy joined the gang.

Tristan laughed. "Of course I'm jealous! I'd never tell Nat, but that is a seriously cool phone."

Natalie gave a shout. Andi sat up on the swing and saw her friend lying flat on her back, fending off three over-excited dogs.

"I think the dogs just got camera shy," Tristan commented. "Hey, Nat! Need a hand?" Natalie managed to push the dogs away and scrambled to her feet.

"At least you'll have gotten some great close-ups," said Andi.

Natalie's mouth twitched. "Yes, I did," she confessed, beginning to laugh. "Especially of Jet's tail!"

They were still giggling when they left the park, taking turns scrolling through the photos on Nat's phone and e-mailing them to their parents and friends.

"Wait," said Tristan, looking around suddenly. "We've gone the wrong way."

"But we only left the park two minutes ago," Andi objected. "How did we get lost so quickly? This is one crazy neighborhood," she added, thinking of how she'd gotten lost on her first walk ever in Orchard Park.

They were standing on a shabby street that she didn't recognize. The buildings looked run-down and uncared for, and there was trash blowing along the sidewalk.

"Where's the tumbleweed?" Tristan joked. "Even my folks would have trouble selling real estate around here."

"We must have come out the wrong end of the park," Natalie guessed.

Buddy whined and pressed against Andi's ankles. Andi knelt down and gave him a reassuring pat. "Are we far from City Hall?" she asked the others.

Tristan pointed along the street. "If we take a left down there, we'll be heading in the right direction. We'll have to loop back around the park."

Andi was relieved to hear that Tristan had a general idea of where they were. She didn't like the vibe she was getting from this area of town. Tristan tugged at Max's leash, but Max seemed reluctant to move. An odd growl had started in the back of the spaniel's throat.

"I've never heard him growl before," Natalie said in surprise. "What do you see, Max?"

Andi noticed a pet store a few doors down the street. Dusty bags were stacked in one window, and the other window was empty — aside from a few small tanks of lizards — allowing for a fairly clear view of the inside.

"It's just a pet store, Max," she said as they approached the shop. "What's there to growl about?"

"Maybe he thinks they're stealing Christine's customers," Tristan quipped.

Max barked again and jumped away, almost tearing the leash from Tristan's hands. Andi had a strange feeling in her stomach as she looked up at the peeling paint on the store front and let her eyes wander to the window. "This isn't a regular pet store," she said. "Look inside! See all those glowing tanks?" She waited while the others carefully peeked inside. "This is a specialty store. And if all the tanks hold what the ones in the front window do, I'd say it's a reptile store." Tristan and Natalie were dumbfounded. "I think you'd better get Max out of here, Tris," she warned. "Something in there is really getting to him."

Tristan pulled Max to the other side of the road, where the spaniel whined uneasily and tucked his tail between his legs.

"There's someone inside," said Natalie, craning her neck to get a better view. "Ughh — It's some guy looking at a huge snake. Sheesh, what is it with people and reptiles in this town?"

All Andi could see was some sandy hair.

"Wait!" Natalie grabbed Andi's arm. "I recognize him. It's that guy who was looking at the snakes in Paws for Thought a couple weeks ago!" she said. "The one who walked out on Tristan's snake speech."

"What are you whispering about?" Tristan called crossly from the far side of the road. "I'm getting a funny feeling that it's something important."

Andi and Natalie backed away from the window. Then they turned to face Tristan and motioned for him to move out of clear view.

"I think," Andi said carefully, "that we just got ourselves another suspect."

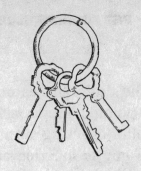

# Chapter Nine

"Don't let him see us," Natalie warned in a loud whisper. "Look, if we stand behind that dumpster, we'll get a good view of the doorway."

They ran back across the road as fast as they dared, gesturing to Tristan to meet them behind the dumpster. Andi half expected the man to come bursting out of the store after them. She felt a bit safer behind the dumpster, though the smell of dirt and rotten food was disgusting. When her heartbeat had slowed a little, she peeked around the side of the dumpster.

Natalie was right. They had a great view of the store, and after a few more minutes the sandy-haired man appeared. He checked his watch, then pulled up the collar of his denim jacket and tucked his hands into the pockets.

"I thought he was a nice guy," Tristan moaned.

"Just because he's into snakes doesn't make him a nice guy," Natalie pointed out. "Don't you think it's a little strange that, after checking out the reptiles at Paws for Thought, this guy is loitering around the reptiles here, too?"

"Tristan," Andi whispered, turning for a moment to look at him, "reptiles are the only animals missing from Christine's store now." A light seemed to go on in his head.

Their attention back on the street, the kids saw the sandy-haired man crossing the road toward them. Andi hissed at the others to stand back and prayed that the dogs would stay quiet — especially Max.

The man walked past the dumpster. Frozen in place, Andi waited for him to turn around and see them, to recognize them — but he walked straight on, his eyes on the road.

"I think I'm going to faint," Natalie whispered shakily.

"Don't you dare," Andi told her, peering after the man. "We can't very well wait around for this guy to rob another store. We've got to follow him!"

"Why follow him and not the lady in sunglasses the other day?" Natalie objected.

"That was a mistake," said Andi, her eyes trained on the man's denim-clad back as he walked farther down the street. "And it's not a mistake I want to make again."

"We haven't got any proof this guy's involved," Tristan protested.

Andi waited until the man was a safe distance ahead of them. "That's why we're going to follow him," she said, and stepped out from behind the dumpster. "If he's innocent, we'll know soon enough."

"You're crazy," Natalie groaned.

"Come on!" Andi beckoned. "He's getting away!"

The man turned down another street. Andi started jogging, anxious not to lose sight of him. What if he had a car? They'd never be able to follow him then.

Running full speed around the corner, Natalie and Tristan nearly collided into Andi's back as she came to an abrupt stop, holding up her hand. Their suspect was leaning down to unlock a bike, barely ten yards away! Scooting back around the corner, they pressed themselves against the wall and concentrated on getting their breathing somewhere around normal again. Andi felt like they were starring in their own cartoon, and had a weird urge to laugh.

"We'll give him two minutes and then follow him, all right?" she said.

"Whatever you say, boss," Natalie said nervously.

Two long, quiet minutes passed. Andi peeped around

the corner again. Their suspect was pedaling slowly up the long hill that led out of town. If it hadn't been for the hill, she had a nasty feeling they would have lost him already.

"I hope you guys are feeling fit," she said, pointing at the hill. "We're in for a long climb."

They set off at a steady pace, with the three dogs trotting beside them. Partway up the hill, Max whined and tugged hard on the leash, his nose pressed hard to the sidewalk.

"Look at Max," Tristan said to the others. "He's acting weird. I wonder if he came this way when he came home last week!"

The sandy-haired man was concentrating on the climb, his head down and his feet pushing hard on the pedals. He didn't look over his shoulder once. As the hill got steeper, Andi realized that all the hours of track-team training she did back in Florida were coming in handy. Even their suspect was taking a break now, getting off his bike to push it along. Looking over her shoulder, Andi saw that the others were lagging behind. Seeing that the man wasn't moving too fast, she stopped to let them catch up.

"My shoes aren't meant for walking this far," Natalie complained, letting Jet pull her up the slope toward

Andi. "My mom bought me these from a cute boutique downtown. They were the last pair." She looked at the scuffed tips of the pale blue Mary Janes. "What am I going to tell her?"

Natalie's mom was always taking her daughter shopping, and, as a result, Nat was one of the best-dressed kids in school. Andi, who would have worn her sneakers to bed if her mom let her, wasn't impressed. "Quit moaning," she said impatiently. "We've nearly caught up with the guy, look!"

Natalie licked her finger and rubbed at the tip of her shoe. "Where is he going, anyhow?" she grumbled.

Andi pointed ahead to where a dark line of trees fringed the horizon. "My guess is that he's heading for the woods," she said. "Where else could you hide a bunch of reptiles and not be noticed?"

Sure enough, they watched their suspect turn his bike at the top of the hill and disappear into the trees. Andi ran to the edge of the woodland as fast as she could, praying that he hadn't vanished into the forest.

A hundred yards along a narrow path stood a small clapboard house, with a small wooden barn attached to the side. The bike was leaning against the gate.

Andi hid behind a tree and watched as the suspect fished out a key and let himself into the house.

"It must be him," Natalie whispered when she and Tristan finally came up behind Andi, out of breath and red in the face.

"How do you know?" asked Tristan.

"Check out the shed," she said, pointing to the barn-like structure to the left of the house.

There, peeking out from under a dark green tarp, its license plate missing, was a silver bumper — attached to the back of what looked like a white van.

Max pricked up his ears at the sight of the vehicle. Like a pro wrestler, Tristan threw himself at the spaniel and clamped his jaw shut before he could bark. "Sorry, Max," he muttered as the dog wriggled furiously. "Silence is a good plan right now."

"We'd better go take a look," Andi said.

But Natalie stopped her. "You've done some crazy things today, but that's the craziest suggestion you've made so far," she warned, putting a hand on Andi's shoulder. "What if he's dangerous?"

"Well, what do you suggest?" Andi demanded.

"We should wait until our suspect goes out again," Natalie said. "Then at least we know we'll have the house to ourselves."

"But that could be ages," Andi moaned. She wanted to get right in there and demand a few answers from the

man. But she knew that Natalie was right. "Okay, you win," she said grumpily.

They settled down at the base of the tree and waited for something to happen. Tristan had three bananas and a couple of granola bars, which they shared. Buddy's tongue was lolling out, so Andi took a bottle of water out of her bag and poured some into the palm of her hand for Buddy and the others to drink. After five minutes, the food and water were all gone.

"Now what?" Andi said, leaning her head back against the tree trunk.

"Let's play I Spy," Tristan suggested.

"Everything will begin with *T*," Natalie groaned, glancing around. "Trees, trees, trees."

To pass the time, they thought of other things around them that began with *T*. Andi was just about to suggest *terrier* when they heard a door slam. They tucked themselves behind the tree as quickly as they could, pulling the dogs in close.

The sandy-haired man locked the front door, looked around briefly, and then climbed onto his bike again. Then he pedaled away down the forest road in a small cloud of dust, away from their hiding place. Andi gave a sigh of relief. She hadn't been sure about how much camouflage their tree was providing.

"Right," she said, looking at the others. "Nat, you stay with the dogs. Tristan and I will take a look around."

"No way are you leaving me out of this," Natalie protested. "I'll take the dogs and go check out the van."

Tristan followed Andi cautiously over to the porch while Natalie and the dogs disappeared into the barn. "He locked the door. What if we can't find a way in?"

Andi stared at the house. It was dilapidated, unpainted, and unloved. There were sure to be rusty hinges on the doors, and perhaps a broken pane of glass. They would find a way in, she was sure of it.

After two minutes of hunting around, she found a window whose latch had entirely rusted through. She pushed it open and peered inside. It smelled of old newspapers and mildew, but the window was just large enough for her to climb through and jump down to the threadbare rug on the floor. Tristan squeezed in after her.

They were standing in a dim little corridor, with a number of closed doors along the two walls and a rickety flight of stairs at the far end. For the first time since they had seen the man outside the store, Andi felt a real twinge of fear. What if he came back? They were just three kids, alone in the woods. Her stomach twisted and she felt a little sick.

"Let me present to you a fine example of Seattle's rural architecture," said Tristan, as if he could tell Andi was starting to get scared. "Enjoy the tranquility of the woods as the trees practically grow up through your floorboards. Immerse yourself in the sound of running water as it flows through your roof."

Andi laughed and felt better. "Come on," she said. "You try that side, and I'll try this one."

The first three rooms were empty. Andi tried the door to a room at the back of the house. The handle rattled in her hand but the door didn't budge. The room was locked.

"The reptiles could be in here," she called over her shoulder to Tristan. "What do we do now?"

Tristan walked over to a small cupboard under the stairs and pushed it open. Sitting on an old iron hook was a set of keys.

"Wow," Andi said, impressed. "How did you know they'd be in there?"

Tristan tried to look modest. "My parents sometimes show clients around houses where the rooms are locked up. The keys are always under the stairs."

Andi tried a couple of keys without success. Then, on the third try, the lock turned with a well-oiled click. She cautiously pushed the door open and found herself looking at a room full of snakes.

*Snakes and lizards*, she corrected herself. And so many! There were at least thirty reptiles in the room. It looked as if Paws for Thought wasn't the only store to have been robbed.

There was a big glowing heater standing in the middle of the room, while glass tanks lined the walls, containing snakes and iguanas and lizards of every color and size imaginable. There was food scattered on the bottom of the tanks — leaves and fruit and a couple of dead things Andi didn't want to check out too closely. The reptiles were mostly curled up and asleep, although one or two turned their scaly heads toward Andi and flicked their tongues at her.

Tristan walked into the room in a daze. "Isn't this the most beautiful thing you've ever seen?" he breathed.

"*Beautiful* isn't the word I would have chosen," Andi admitted. "One or two reptiles are fine, but a whole room of them is kind of creepy."

"It really makes perfect sense," Tristan thought aloud. "The thief took the reptiles, but freed a bunch of the other animals just to throw the police off his trail." He peered into one of the tanks. "There's a python here," he said excitedly. "And a California king snake. And look over there!" He pointed to a large tank in the corner, where two large green reptiles were prowling back and forth. "Mr. Scarpetti's monitor lizards!"

"Here's Christine's corn snake," said Andi, peering into one of the tanks. "She's shed her skin, look!"

The corn snake looked much happier than the last time Andi had seen her. Her scales were smooth and new, and there was a transparent husk of skin lying in the corner of the cage. "That garter snake we found in Mrs. Harper's backyard must not have been interesting enough for this guy," she guessed.

"Or valuable enough," concluded Tristan.

Suddenly, Andi heard the sound of a key in the front door lock. "Quick!" she hissed, looking frantically for somewhere to hide. "He's back! We've got to get out of here."

"Lock the door to the room!" said Tristan. "And put back the key! We don't want to make him suspicious."

With shaking hands, Andi locked the room and hung the key under the stairs. She raced down the corridor to the open window — but it was too late. The front door was already swinging open.

# Chapter Ten

"Hey!" The sandy-haired man looked stunned at the sight of two kids standing in his hallway. "How did you get in here?"

Andi opened her mouth, but no sound came out. The man gave them a sharp glance, then looked across the hall at the locked room. Andi knew he was wondering if they'd seen the reptiles.

"Sorry, mister," said Tristan. He'd given himself a weird accent, and was speaking a little lower than usual. It looked like Tristan didn't want to give the thief any clues that they had met before. "The window was open and, uh . . . Carly here bet me I couldn't get through it."

Andi was impressed with Tristan's quick thinking.

The man narrowed his eyes and stared hard at them. "You're lying," he said, glancing down the corridor at the reptile room again. "Why are you here? What do you want?"

Andi couldn't help it. Her eyes darted toward the closet under the stairs. The thief caught the tiny movement, and strode over to the closet. The keys to the reptile room were still swinging very gently on the hook.

"We can explain," Tristan blurted as the thief swung around with a very unfriendly expression on his face.

"It better be good," the man growled, striding over to the reptile room and unlocking the door. "If anything is missing, you are in serious trouble."

"We, uh, saw the reptiles through the window," Andi improvised in desperation. "And we wanted to take a look. My brother's crazy about snakes. You must be a really cool guy to have so many!"

It was the right thing to say. The man pulled his shoulders back and looked pleased at the compliment. "I guess I've got quite a few," he said gruffly.

Tristan took up Andi's lead. "I've never seen a python before," he gushed.

Tristan's accent was faltering, but Andi knew his enthusiasm was real. Maybe it was enough to get them through this.

The thief swelled a little more. "I know my business," he said. "I got clients all over the world: Europe, Asia,

Australia. They trust that their money will get them good specimens."

"You must be really well-connected," said Andi, wondering desperately how they were going to get out of there. Where was Natalie? Had she seen the thief coming back? Did she have any idea they were stuck in there with him? Andi hoped with all her might that Natalie wouldn't come bounding through the door, unaware the thief had returned.

Tristan was staring at a small speckled rattlesnake in a tank near the window. "Hey Andi!" he said. "Come and take a look at this. Can you believe people keep rattlesnakes as pets?"

Everything went into slow motion as Tristan realized what he'd said. His hand flew to his mouth and his face went white.

"Andi?" said the thief. "I thought you said her name was Carly." His face creased with anger.

At that exact moment, the sharp sound of crunching gravel came from outside. All of them jumped and their heads jerked to the front window. Andi felt like collapsing with relief. The police had arrived!

With barely a glance at Andi and Tristan, the thief raced out of the house, zigzagging left and right as he tried to decide which way to run. But it was use-

less. The police had him completely surrounded. Feeling dazed, like she was in an action movie, Andi watched from the front door as two officers handcuffed the struggling thief and pushed him into a squad car.

"Andi! Tristan!" Christine came running onto the porch. Andi felt like she had never been more pleased to see anyone in her life.

"We were so worried about you all!" Christine exclaimed, giving her a bone-crushing hug. "When Natalie called, we thought we'd never get to you in time." She swung around to Tristan. "Never, *ever* do anything like this again, young man. Your mom would have my guts for guitar strings if she knew what you'd been up to."

Fisher was waiting in the barn with Natalie when Andi and Tristan approached. Christine had one arm wrapped tightly around each of them.

"Thank goodness you're okay!" Natalie gabbled. "I was going crazy, especially when I saw the guy coming back! But I thought of this." She pulled her cell phone triumphantly out of her bag. "I called Fisher as soon as you went inside, and sent him a couple of photos of this place so he'd know where to find us." She glanced smugly at Tristan. "*Now* tell me this phone was a waste of money."

While Fisher checked the reptiles for any health problems, Andi wandered around the house. Now that the thief had been caught, it felt like a different place — cleaner and nicer, somehow.

Walking into the little kitchen at the back of the house, she spotted a worn telephone directory. She flicked through the pages, and a smile spread across her face.

Running back into the reptile room with the directory under her arm, Andi saw Fisher closing the monitor lizards' tank. "Well, at least they've been fed and watered, and their cages are clean," he said, taking off his gloves.

"So he could get a better price for them, I expect," Natalie said, standing back in the doorway and trying not to look too closely at the snakes.

"What I want to know is, where did the rest of these animals come from?" Christine asked anxiously. "I only own eight of these guys. How are we going to find all the other owners?"

Andi waved the telephone directory at Christine. "I found this in the kitchen," she said. "He's circled a number of pet stores in the Orchard Park area — including Paws for Thought."

"Good work, Andi!" said Fisher. "I'll take that back to the ASPCA with me and have our assistants make the calls tonight."

* * *

The police were quick to approach Andi, Tristan, and Natalie about what had happened. They had a lot of questions, but were also determined to explain the seriousness of the kids' actions to them. Without having realized it, Tristan and Andi had come close to "breaking and entering" someone's property, which was quite an offense. Luckily for them, the thief didn't own the run-down cottage and had broken into it himself. Christine had persuaded the cops to let the kids off easy this time, seeing as though they'd only had the best interest of her shop in mind. But it wasn't without some strict reprimanding from each of the officers, first.

The police then proceeded to ask Andi and the others questions about how they had found the thief, who obviously had a nice business going — stealing rare and expensive reptiles from pet stores around the state, and selling them to reptile enthusiasts and collectors overseas. Andi and Natalie kept their answers short, but Tristan couldn't resist going into every detail of his conversation with the thief at Paws for Thought.

"I knew he was trouble the minute I laid eyes on him," he declared, shaking his head and looking solemn. "I told the others, but they didn't listen."

"Not quite the way I remember it, Tristan," said Natalie as they went to help Fisher and Christine load the reptiles into the back of Fisher's van; she stuck to the lizards. "You practically wanted to invite that guy over for a cozy snake sleepover."

Andi held up her hands. "Let's not fight about this, guys," she appealed. "We just caught a thief! How great is that? Let's celebrate!"

She high-fived her friends, and, after a moment's hesitation, they grinned and high-fived each other as well.

"That's it," said Fisher, wiping his hands on his jeans and locking the back of the truck. "So, where to?"

"Back to my place for dinner!" Christine said promptly, ruffling Max's ears as he jumped into the van beside her. "And smoothies all round. With a double topping of strawberries!"

"Music to my ears," Tristan sighed.

Fisher dropped them off at Paws for Thought and helped unload Christine's reptiles from the back of the van. He promised to come back for his smoothie as soon as he had taken the other stolen reptiles over to the ASPCA. "Save some strawberries for me," he called, leaning out of the window as he slipped the van into gear.

"That means no seconds, Tristan," Andi whispered, digging him in the ribs.

But there was no question of fitting in second helpings. Christine produced three enormous tropical fruit smoothies and a plate of sandwiches that even Tristan had difficulty finishing. To their delight, the dogs weren't forgotten in the celebration. Christine cooked them each a juicy sausage.

"I couldn't eat another bite," Tristan sighed, pushing back from the table and resting his hands on his stomach.

"That's something you don't hear very often," Natalie observed, patting her mouth with a napkin and brushing a couple of crumbs off her lap. Andi snorted with laughter.

"You deserve every mouthful," said Christine. "Just promise me you'll never follow a strange man into a forest again."

"We promise," they chorused.

There was the faint sound below of someone coming into the store. They all rushed downstairs and found a pale-faced boy with his mom, and a little girl in a stroller standing by the counter.

"Liam!" Andi exclaimed. "Great to see you! Did you come to get the rabbit?"

Liam looked confused. "I, uh . . . " he said. "I don't know. My mom just said we had to come here."

Mrs. Noble's eyes twinkled. "Thanks for the call, Christine," she said to the pet store owner. "I thought I'd save the news until we got here." She turned to Liam and knelt down. "Honey, I've got some exciting news for you. Would you still like that little gray rabbit for your birthday?"

Liam's eyes grew huge. "You mean I can have her?" he asked in amazement. "You really mean it, Mom?"

Andi watched as Christine reached down behind the counter and produced a traveling cage containing the gray rabbit, who was quietly grooming her long ears. She set it down in front of Liam, who looked as if he couldn't quite believe his eyes.

"Babbit," said the little girl in the stroller, pointing a chubby finger at the cage.

"I figured Lacey was old enough now to understand about pets — " Mrs. Noble began.

"You're the best, Mom!" Liam burst out and flung his arms around her. "This is the best birthday present in the world! I'm gonna call her Smokey, and build her a cage, and everything!"

"I can't believe you ever suspected that kid of robbing the store," Tristan murmured under his breath at Andi.

"And I can't believe your nerve, telling the police you suspected the real thief all along!" Andi countered indignantly.

"And *I* can't believe you're still eating, Tristan," Natalie added, looking at the sandwich in Tristan's hand.

A piece of paper suddenly fluttered out of Tristan's pocket. Andi bent down to pick it up. It was the street plan.

"Hey, I recognize that," said Christine, peering over Andi's shoulder. "It's part of the new plans for parking lots down Main Street. Where did you get it?"

"Parking lots?" Andi echoed.

"Yes," Christine nodded. "We've been designated two new parking spaces! That's what all this construction is for. What did you think?"

"You mean, you *know* about this?" said Tristan, astonished.

"Of course I know about it!" Christine replied. "A lady from City Hall has been over here regularly to explain the plan. I think it's terrific."

Buddy jumped up and snatched the map out of Andi's hand. He put his head between his paws and looked up at Andi, daring her to chase him for the paper.

Andi shook her head and laughed. "Talk about a red

herring," she said, thinking of how convinced they had been that the woman in sunglasses had organized the pet store robbery. It was great being a pet finder, but maybe *everyone's* attention in Orchard Park wasn't quite as animal-focused as theirs!

"*Now* can we return the map to that poor woman?" asked Natalie, looking like she was right all along.

"If you can get it away from Buddy," Andi replied. "It'll be like taking food from Tristan," she said with a smile.

And everyone there laughed — including Tristan.